The Memory of Things

Also by Gae Polisner

THE MEMORY OF THNGS

GAE POLISNER

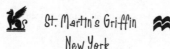 St. Martin's Griffin
New York

THE MEMORY OF THINGS. Copyright © 2016 by Gae Polisner. All rights reserved. Printed in the United States of America. For information, address St. Martin's Press, 175 Fifth Avenue, New York, N.Y. 10010.

www.stmartins.com

The Library of Congress Cataloging-in-Publication Data is available upon request.

ISBN 978-1-250-09552-7 (hardcover)
ISBN 978-1-250-09553-4 (e-book)

Our books may be purchased in bulk for promotional, educational, or business use. Please contact your local bookseller or the Macmillan Corporate and Premium Sales Department at 1-800-221-7945, extension 5442, or by e-mail at MacmillanSpecialMarkets@macmillan.com.

First Edition: September 2016

10 9 8 7 6 5 4 3

To my mother, Ginger, and my father, Stu,
who have always made everything seem possible.

This is your book, Mom. You told me so.

On walls and windows and bins and cars
all around the rubble pile, New Yorkers
have left messages in the grainy dust.
They are expressions of anger, love, despair and
patriotism, a form of temporary poetry that will
last not nearly as long as the memories.

—*LOS ANGELES TIMES,* FROM *TIME WIRE*
REPORTS, SEPTEMBER 16, 2001

She moves in mysterious ways.

—"MYSTERIOUS WAYS," U2, 1991

What was your original face before your
mother and father were born?

—ZEN KOAN

BIRD

I move with the crowd, away from downtown Manhattan.

We travel swiftly but don't run, panicked but steady, a molten lava flow of bodies across the bridge.

A crash of thunder erupts—*another explosion?*—and the flow startles and quickens. Someone near me starts to cry, a choked, gasping sound, soon muted by a new wail of sirens rising at my back.

I stop and turn, stare frozen. People rush past me: faces twisted with shock and fear, mouths held open in O's, others only eyes where their noses and mouths have been covered with knotted sleeves against the toxic, burning reek.

I search for Kristen or Kelly, or Mr. Bell, but I lost them all as soon as we got to the bridge.

I don't see anyone I know from school.

I don't see anyone I know.

I press my sleeve to my nose—*Don't think, Kyle, just move!*—but feel stuck gaping at the place where the city has vanished beyond the thick brown wall of smoke.

Two planes have hit, one building is down, and my dad is in there somewhere.

"Jesus, kid, keep going!" Some guy trips over me and looks back apologetically.

It's only a movie. I'm dreaming.

None of this is real.

"Come on, man! We should get off the bridge!" Another

concerned shove and I'm in motion again, stumbling toward Brooklyn.

My eyes to the ground, I watch my sneakers move forward, one in front of the other, my brain blocked against the sea of smoke, the confetti of steel and glass and paper I watched rain down minutes ago from a fifth-floor window at Stuyvesant.

A fighter jet streaks over us, cutting through the noise in my head.

Walk. Breathe. Don't think about Dad.

When I've almost reached the giant stone pillars that mark the Brooklyn side of the bridge from Manhattan, I finally look up again.

Brooklyn looks clear ahead.

All I need to do is get home.

I push forward, step after step, grasping at song lyrics in my head. I start with the lyrics for "I Will Follow" from *Boy*, one of my all-time favorites, then "Promenade" from *The Unforgettable Fire*—I really have to fish for that one, so it keeps my mind focused, which helps calm me down.

I walk through the guitar chords, wishing I still played, trying to remember the fingering until I get lost in that and fall back in step with the flow. I barely register the wings—*thick with feathers*—of the enormous bird as I pass. It's hunched, curled up into itself, in the shadows of the pillar.

An eagle? A hawk?

No. It was way, way bigger than that.

I glance back as I walk, but I can't see it from here, over the heads of the crowd.

But I know I saw it, crouched near the edge of the bridge.

I walk several more steps, then stop. *What if it's hurt?*

It will only take a few seconds. I feel like I *need* to go back.

I turn and rush toward the pillar as the crowd sweeps forward around me. Someone yells, "Are you nuts, kid?" but my brain keeps seeing the wings.

What if I'm losing it?

What if I only imagined it was there?

I call out, "There was something by the—!" but it's pointless. They can't hear me above all the people and the noise.

I slip through the crowd to my left. A woman catches my sleeve and says, "What are you doing, boy? Don't go back that way!"

I yank free. Something tells me I have to make sure.

A few more feet, and I see it—the bird—pressed against the railing.

Its wings are enormous! I didn't imagine it, then.

As I run toward it, it stands and spreads them wide, leans out, about to take flight.

Blink.

Look down.

Water glistens through steel shadows

        (. . . noise and glass and

                black smoke . . .)

I can float there

        (bodies and blood . . .)

I have wings that will let me

      drift

          down

(. . . the putrid smell of burning skin).
Tilt my face to the sun,
        to the mist,
                and blue sky.
Clear water below.
Spread my wings to
        fly.

"Are you okay?"

I grab at the wing, but I can't get a good hold. White feathers pull free, stick to my fingers, release into the air. My arm shakes uncontrollably as I reach out again.

"Stop!" I yell. "Don't!"

The bird is not a bird, but a girl.

Wait to fall,
        but don't.
Am tethered here.
Turn.
        A boy shouts,
        eyes full of terror.
He grabs hold of me
        (an explosion,
                a ball of fire rising to the sky . . .
                flames
                        everywhere).
Pull away from his grip, but he won't
let go.

She twists toward me, confused, and twists away again.

What is she doing?

The wings are the costume kind my sister might wear for a dance recital or school play, but more elaborate.

I find her sleeve, her arm, dig my fingers in, hold tighter.

My heart pounds so hard it hurts.

Lips move, but no words come.

Twist away, tired

     (so very tired from

        the weight of things).

The boy yells again,

mouth opens,

   and closes.

   Can't hear him.

     (clouds, a glint of

       metal,

         another blast . . .)

Nothing but ringing in my ears.

"It's okay," I whisper, but my fingers dig harder as she tries to pull away. I'm bigger than she is, but I'm afraid I won't be able to hold on. Louder, I say, "Please, it's okay! Let me help you!"

She whips around, eyes wide and blank and scared.

"You can't stay here," I say more softly. She shakes her head but stops struggling, crumples down.

"No," she says, "please." Then something explodes, shaking the bridge.

A bomb? Another building?

"You have to come with me!" I yell. "Now!"

Her eyes search mine, and she lets me pull her up.

I hold on to her sleeve and make her run.

He pulls me along,

says words I can't hear.

Look back to where the clear water sparkles!

        (black scribbles

            blinding heat,

            white light.

      Fire and

           glass spilling

              down.)

"What's your name? Are you hurt?" We've reached the safer, wood-plank part of the bridge. Over land now. Away from the water.

She doesn't fight me anymore, but won't look at me, either.

Here in the bright sunlight, I can study her. Beneath the wings, she wears normal street clothes. Khaki cargo pants, black combat boots, a blue sweatshirt. Her short dark hair is chopped jaggedly, her eyes ringed in heavy black liner. It's hard to tell though, since every inch of her is covered in thick white dust and ash.

Bits of metal glint in her hair.

"Come on," I say, trying to stop shaking and sound calm. "I won't hurt you, I promise. My father is a cop." She walks with me, reluctantly, so slight and fragile under the wings, I could carry her if I needed to.

But I don't. She stays with me. We walk together, toward Brooklyn.

There's no other choice. There's no going back to Manhattan.

Ahead of us, the bridge has almost emptied. At the steps near Cadman Plaza, we head down.

I hold her arm and lead her.

What am I supposed to do?

He walks.

I follow.

He keeps asking things I can't hear

(can't think, can't breathe,

. . . can't find you . . .)

Nod,

follow,

walk.

His words disappear.

We move away from the bridge, the stream of sirens—fire engines, police cars, ambulances—all fading into the distance.

I take a deep breath, then another, my thoughts spiraling everywhere.

Two planes have been flown into buildings like bombs. *What if there are more? What makes us think it's over?*

And what about Dad? He's Joint Terrorist Task Force, the first guys sent in during a crisis.

He'll be okay, right?

It's his job. He has to be okay.

I try to distract myself by asking the girl questions, but she doesn't answer and, in the silence, my brain spirals uncontrollably again.

Mom and Kerri! They were supposed to come home today! Fly the fuck home from California.

What if they are in a plane? They could be in the air right now!

What time were their flights? Christ! Why can't I remember what time?

There's another boom, and I yank us to the ground. A second fighter jet streaks by overhead.

When it's gone from earshot, I find my cell phone, thinking I'll try to reach Mom, then almost laugh, realizing.

"I was going to call my mother," I say, my voice shaking, "but she doesn't have a cell phone."

The girl nods, and her eyes shift to mine for a second, then move past me and stare off at nothing. I don't know if she's listening, but I ramble on nervously anyway. "She says she hates cell phones, and that she's going to be the last holdout on Earth. And my sister is too young to have her own."

The girl doesn't respond.

Jesus, maybe I should have just left her there.

I pull her up and start walking again, obsessed with reaching my mother, wracking my brain for the name of the place where they have been staying all summer. The Something Something Garden Apartments in LA.

I should know it. It's been up on the fridge for weeks. Scrawled in my mother's handwriting.

I check the time on my phone. 10:40 A.M. here, which means it's three hours earlier there. What are the chances their flight would leave that early?

They're probably still sleeping.

They probably don't even know.

I jam my phone back in my pocket, wondering if I should try Dad instead. But I know better. He will be down there. *In* there.

A hard lump swells in my throat.

I'm sure he'll call me when he can.

Strange streets,
   strange signs:
      Cranberry,
         Orange,
            Pineapple.
      (A brick terrazzo with fruit trees in
                blue glazed pots . . .)
A loud bang, and
   we're down on the ground.
   The boy says something to me:
      ". . . call my mom . . .
      she hates them . . ."
When he pulls me up,
   we walk faster.

Manny, my favorite doorman, has his eyes glued to the television when I enter. He must have the news on. I'm relieved to be home, and relieved he's distracted.

You can't see the television from here; it's a small portable one that sits below the counter of the desk. But I know it's there because, normally, he feeds Yankees scores to me when I come in.

"You okay, Mr. Donohue?" he asks, not looking up completely. I want to stop and ask questions about what's going on, but I nod curtly instead and usher the girl past and toward the elevators. I don't want to explain her. I have no clue how.

She stays close, so I act like she's some school friend despite how crazy she looks. Despite her hair, and the ash, and the wings.

"Yeah, I think so, thanks."

I push the up button.

"Shame," Manny murmurs behind me. "You never think this happen in our country."

In the elevator, I press eleven and tap the *close door* button repeatedly. The bird girl keeps her eyes averted.

When the doors finally shut, I fumble with my phone, eyeing her cautiously. Now that we're in close quarters, I feel awkward and at a loss for words. "I should try my dad," I say. "He's probably down there . . ." The words catch in my throat.

On my phone, the message light is flashing. Maybe it's him telling me everything will be okay.

"Just so you know, my mom is away, but my uncle is upstairs. He's a mess, though," I add, figuring I should warn her.

Then again, maybe it's my uncle who needs warning.

The elevator lurches up. I try to stay calm as I play the message, my father's solid voice filling my ears.

"Kyle, listen . . ."

That's it. The message cuts off. I can't tell what time it's from. I play it again, but it's the same thing: those two words, and he's gone.

I try not to lose it, not to cry. Maybe I don't have reception in here.

Or, maybe he doesn't have reception where he is.

Or, maybe . . . *fuck.*

I snap my phone closed as the elevator doors open, and step out onto our floor with the girl.

The hallway is quiet,
beige,
     smells of something faint,
    but familiar:
        Coffee.
        New carpet.
        Scrambled eggs.
A light fixture flickers overhead.
            (a hospital corridor . . .
                    a buzzing florescent . . .)
The boy stops and faces me at the third door.
11C.
"This is us."
    Sound, returning.
"I'm Kyle, by the way," he says.

My hands shake so badly it makes it hard to get my key in the lock. When I finally do, I stand with the door half open, because now there's another message flashing on my phone.

How did I miss the call?

I press the phone to my ear, holding a finger up for the girl to give me a second. Dad's voice is urgent, but steady.

"Kyle, I hope you can hear me . . . It's chaos down here . . ." Whatever he says next is drowned out by the rise and fall of sirens, then, ". . . no way to keep calling . . . hard to get through. I just wanted to . . . I'll call you back, son. I have to go in . . ."

There's a bang. Things crashing. More sirens. Sounds muffled as Dad loses his grip on the phone. Terrified, I try not to flinch, to cry. Cold washes over me as I pray for his voice to return. Even when it breaks through again, I can't stop shivering.

". . . I'm going to assume all is okay with you . . . that you're home or safe, and that they've evacuated your school." He sounds clearer now, unbroken, as if he's moved to somewhere he can talk.

"And, Kyle, I haven't reached your mother yet . . . Let her know, and call me when you get home. Or wherever it is they send you. Listen to me, Kyle. Don't call first. Get somewhere safe, *then* call. Jesus Christ . . . !" Another crash, and someone yells in the background. The frantic sound of sirens picks up again. Dad's voice returns, but it's hard to hear. "Okay, I've got to go. Call me when you get where you're going. Leave a message if you have to. And wait there till I get home. Nothing stupid, you hear me, son? Safe and smart. And please call."

He hangs up. There are no more messages.

I know I need to calm down.

I look at the girl. Her eyes dart away.

Nothing to do but go inside.

The boy—Kyle—
turns to me,
     eyes searching.
          (. . . search for you . . . white noise . . .)

I look away.

(bodies,

fall . . .)

Don't ask me.

I don't even know why I'm here.

I step inside, relieved to be home, but it's weird to have this girl here with me.

I don't know what I should do with her.

The apartment is quiet. I need to check on Uncle Matt, reach Dad, locate Mom, check the news.

But first, the girl. She needs to get washed up. She can't stay in our apartment covered in all that ash.

"Come." I lead her down the hall to the bathroom, pointing out Kerri's room on the way. "You can shower, then use my sister's room to change when you're done. To rest. Whatever you want," I say. "And leave your stuff on the washer." I hand her a fresh towel. "I'll find you something to wear while I clean those."

She nods, and I start to close the door, spotting my father's straight razor on the sink. With Uncle Matt staying here and sharing Dad's bathroom so much, Dad uses ours more and more.

What if she really was going to jump? To kill herself?

I can't just leave those there.

I grab two washcloths from the cabinet, use one to swipe the razor from the edge, leaving the other one there for her to use.

I close the door.

The lock clicks behind me.

If she was going to kill herself, what was I thinking bringing her here?

I bury the razor in a wastebasket in the hall, and carry the wings—*freaking wings, are you kidding me?*—out to the small terrace off my parents' bedroom, and shake them off as best I can while staring south at the sky.

From here, it is clear and blue—a normal day, but for the acrid burnt smell that has already made its way across the river.

It chokes me, making my eyes tear up. I need to focus and keep moving.

But now that I'm home, I feel stuck in slow motion.

I head back inside, closing and locking the terrace door. Everything feels off. Everything seems foreign and wrong.

We've been attacked, right? So, does this mean we're at war?

In Kerri's room, I pick up speed, hanging the wings over the back of the desk chair, trying to find the girl something to wear. But everything my sister owns is pink and sparkly, like it's been puked from the closets of Disney.

I run to my room instead, find a pair of pajama pants from a few years ago, plaid with a drawstring so she can tighten them. I dig out my prized U2 PopMart Tour T-shirt Uncle Matt got me for my fifteenth birthday, also too small on me now, and lay those out on top of my sister's bed.

There. Good enough.

It's not like she's staying.

It's not like she'll need them for long.

OPEN WINDOW

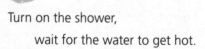

Turn on the shower,
　　wait for the water to get hot.

In this room:

> Sink,
>> washcloth,
>> medicine cabinet,
>> washing machine,
>> dryer.
>> Magazine basket,
>>> pink robe.

None of it feels like mine.

Breathe,
> stare in the
>> steamed-up mirror.

Wipe the glass with my hand,
> but nothing
>> comes clear.

I race to the kitchen and grab the scrap of paper from the fridge.

In Mom's handwriting: *Chase Knolls Garden Apartments. Suite 4B.*

I should have remembered Chase Knolls.

I dial the number but get a busy signal; redial, same thing. It's the fast kind of busy like the number is broken.

The circuits must be jammed. Everyone is trying to reach someone.

I slip the paper back under the magnet and dial my dad instead. He *said* to, and I really need to hear his voice, but that call doesn't go through, either.

I dial Chase Knolls again, frantic, and stand against the counter listening to the endless beeping in my ear.

Eyes closed,
the warm water soothes.
                 (The smell of vanilla,
                         sweet and familiar . . .)
Suds slip down
     my skin
                         (. . . tubes, blood . . .
                             shattering glass . . .)
but nothing can rinse it all
                 away.

I hear Kerri's door close down the hall.

Maybe this is all some really crazy weird dream, the kind you wake yourself from and laugh because you dreamed it was a dream within the dream.

On the bed: plaid pajama pants
                 and a blue T-shirt with an
                         upside-down planet on it.
I pull them on.
The shirt
     hangs from me,
             (. . . wasting away . . .)
     same as the pants.
I sit on the bed and wait,
             the heat, the shirt, the room,
             all making me squirm.

I knock on my sister's door, wait, then open it.

The girl sits on the bed in my stuff, all of it way too big.

For a second, I'm stunned. She looks totally different clean and showered, eyeliner gone, jagged hair wet and smoothed down. Under all that ash, her face is still tanned from summer, pink-cheeked from the hot shower, and her wide-set eyes are deep brown and warm. Up close they have cool amber flecks in them.

She looks sweet and lost. She looks pretty. And scared.

"Was the shower okay?" I look away, self-conscious, then back again. She nods. "That stuff okay?" I indicate the clothing, and she shrugs. "It's big, I guess. I'll try to find you something better in a bit." She nods again, and I walk in far enough to take the wet towel from her trembling hands.

Kyle stands there.
He doesn't seem like anyone I know.
    "Okay?
Okay?
    Okay?" he asks.
I can't answer,
    I'm not here,
        I'm crawling out of my own
            skin.
He waits, so I try,
      nod and breathe past the
        scraping pieces in my chest:
          (brick,
            stone,

metal,
glass).

Try to ignore how it aches.

"Okay, I'll leave you be, then," I say.

She stares out my sister's window. My eyes follow. From this angle, all you can see is blue sky.

"Maybe rest for a while. I have to talk to my uncle, let him know that you're here. I have to reach my mom, too. I'll put your clothes in the washer and come back again."

He closes the door.
The purple room hurts my head.
    Purple rug. Lavender walls. Purple curtains.
Out the window,
    the tops of apartment buildings
            (a second glint of metal
                    breaks through the clouds . . .).
    Wires,
        blue sky,
Brooklyn Heights, he had said.
I walk to the window,
        unlock it,
                and
            pull.

I'm about to throw in the load of wash, but instead I turn back to my sister's room and crack the door open without knocking.

I nearly freak. The girl stands at the window, which is open. Only partway, though, because of the window guards.

"Sorry," I say, startling her. "Are . . . are you sure you're okay?" She turns, wide-eyed, and blinks. "I won't bug you anymore, but I figured I should know your name."

She stares blankly.

"What I should call you, I mean."

She steps away from the window, and I relax a little.

"I don't know," she finally says.

When he leaves, I try again,
but the window only opens
                a few inches.
I back away,
defeated.
He said to rest, but I don't feel tired.
            I feel
                strange and
                        on edge.

I sit on the bed and stare down at
                the ruffled pillow,
                the white comforter with its hideous
                    black, pink, and purple design.
                    Stars and music notes repeat across it,
                    and movie things:
                    black clapboard slates with white letters that
    read,

ACTION!

TAKE!

ROLL SCENE!

Across the pillowcase:

BE THE STAR YOU ARE.

This is not my room.

I'm in a story I know from elsewhere.

(A girl comes to a cabin in the woods,

eats porridge,

sits in three different chairs,

sleeps in the wrong beds.

"This porridge is too hot . . .

this porridge is too cold . . .")

Words that move on a conveyer belt through my gauzy head.

I stumble out of Kerri's room and down the hall.

How can she not know her name?

Jesus. She's not only suicidal, she has no memory. Maybe she hit her head and blacked out. I should take her somewhere, but where? I'm too afraid to go out there right now, and, anyway, the hospitals are going to be filled with wounded people. Besides, she doesn't seem hurt. Or look hurt. She's not fainting or bleeding, or—I don't know. My stomach twists. I need to take her somewhere, anywhere that's not here.

I need to reach my parents.

I need to check the news.

But first, I have to deal with Uncle Matt.

A poster of three
            long-haired boys.
        I close my eyes against them,
        against their girlish hair and the bright yellow background.
            (Flashes of sunlight . . .
                    long black strands scattered
                            across
                a worn linoleum floor . . .)
    I shift my weight on the bed.
            The Three Bears trudge across my brain.

The door to the guest room, where Uncle Matt sleeps, is closed. I open it slowly. I won't know what to say if he's seen the news.

Worse, I won't know what to say if he hasn't.

This I know: It will kill him either way. It will devastate him not to be down there with his unit, doing his job. Down there with Dad and Uncle Paul.

My heart bangs in my ears as I search for the right thing to say. What to tell him first. How to break news I don't understand.

How to explain about the planes, and the building, and the girl.

But he's asleep in his wheelchair, head down, in front of the television. I can tell by the way his body slumps to the side.

Usually when I get home from school, Karina has dressed him, bathed him, and moved him into the living room. But Karina never made it here this morning.

The television is on, but the volume is muted.

He doesn't know yet. If he knew, he wouldn't be sleeping.

My eyes freeze on the images—the falling building, the wall of white smoke filling the screen, the people running from the South Tower collapsing, over and over again—then shift to the news crawl at the bottom of the screen. It says the North Tower collapsed. A mistake. It was the South Tower. I watched it go down.

I back out of the room, pulling the door shut, hoping Uncle Matt will stay asleep for a while more. Closing my eyes, I rest my head against the door.

But the images keep coming.

On the ceiling,
    a dull wink of stars.
      The plastic glow-in-the-dark kind,
        in daylight, the color of
          old teeth.
I close my eyes and count backward
    100 . . . 99 . . . 98 . . .
Numbers, clear and
    exact,
don't require me to think.
      97 . . . 96 . . . 95 . . .
I remember the shower,
    the elevator,
    and
    the bridge.
      94 . . .

I remember the boy.
> 93 . . .

Kyle.
> Everything before him goes blank.

Watch the old-teeth stars and
> keep counting,
>> 92 . . . 91 . . . 90 . . .

This bed is too soft.

The North Tower, the news said. What if that one went down, also?

I walk to the living room and stand, useless, not wanting to look out the window.

I dial Dad—busy signal—then try the Chase Knolls apartments again.

Busy signal.

How am I supposed to reach anyone?

I leave my phone on the couch and walk back to the kitchen. Maybe the landline will work better. I dial Dad first—still busy—but the Chase Knolls call rings through!

A machine picks up and tells me to dial 0 if I'd like to leave a message for a guest.

Fuck!

I head to the bathroom, trying to steady myself, telling myself to get things done and not to worry. Mom is far from the attacks, and Dad is trained to deal with exactly these types of situations.

The washer is mid-cycle, so I walk back to the living room, find the remote, and turn on the television. The ticker still shows the North Tower.

I brave it and turn, look out the big picture window with a view of the East River, but through all the smoke, I can't see a thing in downtown Manhattan.

The explosion on the bridge.

Was that the North Tower going down?

Jesus, what if my dad was in there?

"YOU . . . DAH . . ."

I flip channels. They all show the same thing. One building imploding, then the other.

On channel after channel, the buildings collapse. People run from them, away from a barreling wall of white smoke.

If my dad was in there, he'd have been trying to rescue people. There's no way he would have run.

A reporter breaks in, holds a hand to her ear and nods as if she's learning new information. She ticks off things that have happened since this morning. Both towers are down, and the Pentagon has been hit. And a hijacked plane has crashed in a field in Pennsylvania.

"We believe it may have been headed for the White House," the reporter says, her eyes full of panic and tears. "So it's a blessing," she adds, but can't finish. The freaking news reporter is crying.

"We're hearing reports—we don't know how many other targets are in danger. Military jets have been scrambled," she says, pulling herself together, "dispatched to head off flights around the country." She nods at whatever is being said in her ear, then adds, "I . . . forgive me . . . I've just been told they've been issued the authority to shoot down planes from anywhere within the United States."

FUCK. My mom and sister might be up there.

I dial the Chase Knolls apartments frantically again, listen to it ring and ring, listen to the message pick up, and dial 0 as told, to leave a message for a guest.

"Please," I say. "A message for suite Four B, Alyse Donohue. She's staying there with my sister. Please ask her to call me. This is Kyle. I'm in New York. I'm her son."

I hang up, press my face to the living room window, and squint out again at the East River. Police boats cover the surface, their red lights flashing through the smoke like in some movie. I don't remember ever seeing a police boat on the river.

On the television, the reporter is in motion, walking swiftly, saying how they need to move their operations, that the local stations are losing their signals because three of the network's transmitters have been lost. "They were on top of the North Tower. Whole communications towers are out. People are struggling to reach their loved ones." She pauses and looks intently into the camera: "So, we're asking our viewers— begging—that if you don't have to make a phone call, you don't."

I turn my gaze north toward upper Manhattan, where Marcus lives. I was going to call him and make sure he got home. I haven't talked to him since we left Mrs. Bright's classroom. He would have headed uptown with another teacher when Mr. Bell took us to the bridge. I guess I'm not calling him now.

Up there, at least, just a few miles from the towers, the sky is deceptively clear. Like it was when I woke up this morning.

A million what-ifs bounce around in my head just as the reporter says something about another flight being hijacked and going down.

"Let me retract that," she corrects immediately. "We don't have a confirmation on that yet."

I reel back from the window, but even inside our apartment there's no escaping any of it. A faint burnt smell seems to cling to the air. Plastic. Rubber. *Jesus, I don't want to know what else.*

Or maybe it's me. Maybe the smell is stuck to my clothes. I'm doing nothing useful here. I should go shower also.

A door closes, opens, then closes again.
Each small bang makes me jump inside my skin.
The shower runs.

    The long-haired boys gawk at me from the wall.
Out the window, clouds bob on blue sky.
    Behind my lids: a hospital bed.

        Faces slip past,

            mere shadows.

     Names and objects

        like skittish

    eye floaters,

        threatening to slip in from

          beyond

          the periphery.

The shower is good, makes me feel more relaxed. Mom always says that after laughter, water is the best medicine.

Mom.

I tell myself she'll be okay.

Her. My sister. And Dad.

One thing I know about Dad: He's a badass. If anyone can walk out of there, he can.

Then again, Uncle Matt was a badass, too, and look at him now.

The shower still runs.
I wander out of the purple room and
                down the hall
                        to the master bedroom.
It's neat and pristine:
                White bedspread with a paisley design.
                Blue curtains.
                A framed painting of flowers in a vase.
                        (. . . Pink peonies . . .
                                everything shattered . . .)
A master bathroom,
        cluttered.
                A toilet equipped with rails.
                On the sink, a parade of pill bottles.
I pick them up, one
        by one:
                        Ketorolac Tromethamine,
                        Celebrex,
                        Coumadin,
                        Tylenol—Codeine,
                        Valium.
I slip the last bottle in my pocket,
        shaking it first,
to be sure.

I dry off, change into clean clothes from the basket next to the dryer, and head back to the living room, noting Kerri's closed door as I pass.

I sit and stare at the television. The reporter from earlier is gone, replaced with a new one.

On the couch, my cell phone message light flashes. I pick it up and listen, happiness filling me as Mom's voice filters in.

"Oh my gosh, Kyle, honey, I can't believe I got through. Call me. It's all over the news . . ." Not surprisingly, she's freaking out. Okay, so maybe I am, too. I can barely hear her over my own heart pulsing in my ears. ". . . I need you to call me. I tried your father but can't reach him. Kyle, please . . . call me here as soon as you can . . . Oh, shoot . . . the number is . . ." She fumbles for something, says, "Kerri, give it to me! Please," then reads off some number I don't recognize. "We're at LAX. Our flight was supposed to leave in an hour. I didn't even know until . . ." Her voice trails off, and she starts to cry. Finally she whispers, "Well, clearly it's not leaving now."

Relief! I want to cry with it, knowing they're not in the air.

The message ends. Already, there's a new one flashing. God, let this one be Dad.

"Kyle, honey?"

It's Mom again, not Dad.

"I didn't mean to hang up. Jesus, I hate these things. Kerri, what am I doing wrong here?" There's a high-pitched beep in my ear. She's still pushing buttons, doesn't realize it's already gone through to my voice mail.

I hear my sister yell: "No, not that one, Mom! I told you that one hangs it up . . ." and they're gone again.

I replay the first message, run to the kitchen to write the number down, letting a third message play, praying with all my might that it's Dad.

"Kyle, sorry, it's me again. If you're getting these, if you're listening, I'm sure your father is down there—already down there . . . I'm sure he knows more than we do. But it's just . . . I can't reach him . . ."

There's a choked sound, and Kerri yells, "Mom! Stop! Tell him what you need to!" and her voice steadies again.

"Anyway, we're going to get home to you as soon as we can. But I don't know . . . if you can reach your father . . . I just need to know that you're both okay. So, call me, please. I'm borrowing this nice man's phone—Ed, his name is Ed. I swear if it's the last thing I do, I'm getting a cell phone when we get home. Wait, okay, here's the number again."

She repeats the number I've written down and says, "We're going to try to get out of here, find somewhere to stay, a hotel or something. If we leave, I'll try you as soon as I can. Or call this phone. I'll leave Ed our information . . . Wait, Kerri, it's beeping! Maybe it's him! How do I answer this thing?"

There's a click, and she's gone.

I stare at the phone, waiting for it to ring, trying to figure out why I didn't hear the other calls, but probably nothing is coming through the way it should.

I dial the number Mom left me for Ed, but that doesn't go through, either.

I toss the phone down and walk to the fireplace, to the row of framed photographs on the mantel. There aren't any recent ones, only one from my parents' wedding, another of Dad when he made Lieutenant, and a third of me holding Kerri as a baby. There are a few more of Kerri, including one on a swing, and another in a school play dressed as Tinker Bell.

I pick up that one and stare at Kerri's little white wings, thinking of the girl's wings. Kerri wore a pair like that for something else, too. A Christmas play. A recital. A dance thing where she played an angel.

I stare back at the wedding photo, at my mom. At my dad. We look alike, he and I, but I'm not much like him. He'd like me better if I were.

Still, I've never wanted him to get back home so bad.

In the sister's room, I stand at the cracked-open window,
                feel for the bottle in my pocket.
I don't have a glass of water.
I listen for the shower, but
        it's already off,
        so
        I can't go get one now.

Dad's phone finally rings!
Then it rings and it rings and it rings.
I pick up another photo of Dad, this one with Uncle Matt and Uncle Paul. They're at the base of a ski slope in Vermont. I should try calling Uncle Paul. He can be a jerk, but maybe I can reach him. I'm worried about him, too. I'm worried about everyone.

I put the photo back and think about Uncle Matt, how he's different from both Dad and Uncle Paul. Tough but nice, and crazy smart. Before his accident he was a lieutenant in the Emergency Service Unit.

"All Donohue men are cops, Kyle . . ." Uncle Paul's words drum in my ears. Every Thanksgiving he starts in on me, worst was the year I decided to switch to Stuyvesant.

"What's wrong with Brooklyn Tech? Too tough for you? Am I wrong, Tom? Why is my nephew going to a sissy school?"

"It's a science and math school, Uncle Paul."

"All pansies, I say! A bunch of freaks and geeks and nerds."

This November, if we all live that long, I'm sure he'll be at it again.

Honestly, I'm used to it, but it makes me miss the old Uncle Matt even more. He'd always defend me, put Uncle Paul in his place.

Uncle Matt. I should check on him again. Wake him up. Tell him what's happened, and about the girl.

For a second, I think about leaving the last part out, my brain plotting some ridiculous sketch comedy routine instead. Like from some old sitcom or movie. For the next twenty-four hours, I wheel an oblivious Uncle Matt around the apartment, to any place the girl isn't, never letting him see her in the halls. She goes along with the scheme, ducking behind couches and potted plants (cue canned laughter), tiptoeing past as I wheel Uncle Matt in circles to avoid spotting her. Finally, we slip her out the front door, Uncle Matt never the wiser that she was ever here (cue cheesy music).

As I'm about to go, I notice I put the wedding photo back up crooked and walk to straighten it, wishing I would get an update from Mom.

She's been in LA since July. She and Kerri should have been

back last week, but then Kerri got some sort of callback for an audition. My dad had balked about her missing the start of school, but Mom had won the fight, as always, saying it was a once-in-a-lifetime chance.

I think Uncle Matt not doing better is the main reason Mom went to California in the first place, agreeing to accompany Kerri so she could attend some dumb acting camp there all summer. She couldn't watch Uncle Matt waste away any longer, so she hired Karina full-time and pays her with her money, at least whatever amount the NYPD doesn't cover. Either way, I'm not naive, I know Mom is the one who wanted Uncle Matt to stay here with us, and she's the one with the money. A trust-fund baby. Which is how we live in a four-bedroom apartment in Brooklyn Heights with a view of the East River. Not exactly affordable on a cop's salary.

Before she left, I heard Dad telling her that we'd need to move Uncle Matt out of here by the end of the year. "It's not practical, Alyse. We're not properly equipped, Karina or not. You know it's not good for him, or us, to keep him here."

As if hearing my thoughts, Uncle Matt calls out—"Ky-uh!"—some sad, pathetic grunt that may be my name, or may be Karina's, or may not even be a real word.

I lie down,
        stare up at old-teeth stars,
    then
close my eyes, and
try to sleep.

On a stage, a heavy curtain rises,
        revealing a
        shimmering lake.
Cautiously, I
   wade in
   and glide across its smooth surface.
Water ripples where I pass,
       swirls into eddies that
          widen into deeper,
            bottomless
              circles.
I stop, adrift.
   A bottle appears in my hand.
       I open it,
       tip it over, and
       spill out the pills.
    White dots spin and disappear
          into the vortex.
I cup my hands to the water and drink,
   waiting for everything to go numb.

Sated, I watch for you
     on the far shore.
   "Here!" you call, and I smile,
    move through the water to
       where you are.
But, thunder crashes,
        a cacophony of cymbals
and the sky darkens.

Rain falls in sheets,
        filling my mouth, and
        the lake sucks me under.

I crack the guest room door open. Uncle Matt is sitting upright. Well, a little more upright than before. He's watching the news.

"Uncle Matt," I say softly, trying not to startle him. "You saw . . ."

"Ky-uh." I move closer. "Jes-uh . . . fugh-ing . . . Christ . . ."

"I know." His head twitches toward the television. He doesn't turn to see me, because he can't. "I know," I repeat. "It's . . . crazy." I have no words strong enough for what it is.

I squat in front of him so he can see my face. Beyond his bed, the room is a mess of physical-therapy equipment: bands and balls and straps and other torture devices, all courtesy of the NYPD and Mom. "I'm sorry," I say. "I came in here and checked on you earlier, but you were still sleeping, and, well, Karina didn't make it in."

"You . . . dah . . . ?" He's not mincing words, then.

"In there, in the mess, I'm guessing. I heard from him earlier, but not since the second tower went down."

"Ih . . . bah . . ." he says, head bobbing.

It's bad.

"Yeah, I know."

"How . . . bou . . . you . . . mah?"

"She's okay, I think. She and Kerri are stuck at the airport in LA. Or were. They never got on the plane . . ." My voice breaks, but I can't lose it right now, not in front of Uncle Matt.

"They're safe, though. She called and said they'll call again when they find a hotel. But I'm worried about Dad." I nod at the television. "They keep saying there may be more planes . . ." Uncle Matt makes an unintelligible sound. "They've grounded all flights. Said they'll shoot them down," I add.

"Gah . . . dayh . . . fuh-ghurs . . ." he says.

I close my eyes for a second, dizzy. I still have to tell him about the girl. But then what? "Dad said in his message to stay here. To stay put. And to take care of you until he gets home." I'm about to mention the girl but quickly change my mind, kick up the lock on his wheelchair, and roll him backward to maneuver him out. It's too much. I can't do it yet, unload about some suicidal amnesiac bird girl that I brought here, to our home. Now. In the middle of all this.

"Wai . . . Ky-uh . . ." He nods with effort back toward the television.

He wants to watch the breaking news. Onscreen a reporter stands in a field in front of a plane, nose down, jutting up from the ground like a crashed missile. Behind it: a smoking crater in the grass, burnt metal parts, a whole wing. The news crawl reads: SHANKSVILLE, PENNSYLVANIA . . . UNITED AIRLINES FLIGHT 93 . . .

"They hit the Pentagon, too," I say. "They think that one was headed toward the White House, but they don't know for sure."

"You . . . dah . . ." he says again. He's worried, and I am, too.

"Yeah," I say, "I'm trying to reach him, Uncle Matt, I promise. I don't know what else to do. It's either busy or rings and rings. If he's in there . . . Well, you know. If he's in there, he's working. Even if he's okay, there's no way he's going to pick up."

The reporter disappears, and the screen returns to the image of people running from the barreling wall of white smoke. I move Uncle Matt out now, and he doesn't argue. He must have to use the bathroom pretty bad.

I wheel him down the hall, past Kerri's closed door, wishing I could just blurt it out about the girl. Get it over with. It's the least of our problems right now. But, I don't. I don't know why, but I can't.

At the end of the hall, I veer to my parents' bedroom, toward the master bathroom with the special rails. I'm nervous—I've never done this alone—but what choice do I have? I haul Uncle Matt out of his chair, get his sweats down, and heave him onto the toilet seat, securing the rails.

It's no easy feat, and I'm sweating by the time I'm done.

"You okay?" He nods, and I avert my eyes. "I'll give you some privacy, then. I'll come back and get you in a few."

". . . Je . . . su . . . fugh-ghers . . ." I hear him mutter as I close the door.

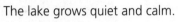

The lake grows quiet and calm.
        The sky lightens,
                though a few drops of mist still fall.
                        They break the water's surface with a
                        delicate *plink plink*
                                (the drip of an intravenous . . .)
                        leaving ripples as they

disappear.
The sun swells from behind a cloud,
and the lake
    evaporates,
      leaving the stage
          empty
    and
        silent.
Nothing but air
        (wings
    and
         bone).

ZEN KOANS

The washer has stopped, and the bathroom smells of clean laundry. There is something so soothing about the scent.

Since Mom left for LA, laundry's pretty much been my job. I don't mind doing it. It's one thing I kind of do well.

I pull the girl's things out one by one. A long-sleeved gray shirt with pinprick holes in the fabric. Khaki cargo pants. A navy blue hooded sweatshirt. A pair of black bikini underwear with little blue bows on the sides. A white lace bra.

My ears burn red as I lay the bra on top of the dryer. I place the other pieces inside. I try not to think of the girl in my sister's bed, nothing between my clothing and her skin. I try not to think of her this morning, leaning out over the bridge.

Was she really going to jump?

I remember Uncle Matt telling a story once about some

distraught guy they rescued off the Brooklyn Bridge. That's the kind of stuff his unit does. It was broad daylight, and people were just walking by him. They said he had stood there so long, nobody thought he was serious. Finally someone called the cops, and they saved him. But, a week later, they found him dead somewhere else. On the West Side Highway, I think. Uncle Matt had said that if you ever wanted to off yourself, the Brooklyn Bridge was the best place to do it, that only one person had ever survived that jump. Some guy a long time ago who had practiced the right way to fall.

I shift the bra again so it lies flat, knowing not to dry it from when Kerri got her first real bra last winter. Daily announcements had ensued about its care and handling, as if a little shrinkage wouldn't have helped things.

I'm about to turn the dryer on but decide to double check that the stuff is really clean. I pull the girl's shirt out and hold it, damp, to my nose. Sure enough, below the Tide fresh ocean scent, the faint smell of smoke lingers. Maybe I should put it all back through again, or maybe it doesn't matter how many times I wash it.

I toss the shirt back in, set the knob to permanent press, and wait for the motion to start, then stand listening to the dryer's rhythmic hum. Wet pieces slump against the metal walls. A faint metallic sound *pings* every third rotation or so. I yank the door open and reach around to see what's making the sound, but I don't find anything, so it must be a button or a zipper. Still, I change my mind anyway, pull everything out, and switch it back into the washer again. I add another scoop of detergent and set it on the longest, hottest cycle.

After I shut the empty dryer, I sit and stare at my reflection in its glass. The face that looks back is my dad's. How can I look so much like him and not feel at all like we're the same?

What was your original face before your mother and father were born?

One of Mrs. Bright's Zen koans pops into my brain. Zen koans are riddles that don't have any right answers. Like the famous one about one hand clapping, or the tree that falls in the forest when no one is around. We've been discussing them in class, together with J. D. Salinger's *Nine Stories*.

But the one in my head, about your original face, I kind of get, suddenly. It's like wondering if you exist at all outside of how your parents view you, without their expectations of how you'll turn out.

I get up and head out of the bathroom, but then I see the girl's combat boots by the door. Black leather, under a thick white layer of ash.

She must have been right there *at* the towers because, only a few blocks away, I wasn't covered nearly this bad.

I wipe them down with a wet soapy washcloth at the sink, walk to my sister's room, and listen for noise inside. When I don't hear any, I leave the boots outside her door.

I sit up, drenched in sweat.
      (RUN! Go now!)
   But go where?
   I don't know where I am
         or where I belong.

I close my eyes,
grip the bottle in my pocket,
and try to sleep some more.

Before I get Uncle Matt from the bathroom, I dial Dad again.

"Don't do anything dumb," he had said, and yet, too late. I already have. There's a suicidal, amnesiac bird girl down the hall.

On Gold Street, not too far from here, there's a precinct. If it's safe to go out later, maybe I'll bring her over there.

I get the rapid busy signal and redial, and this time his voice mail answers.

Hearing his voice on the recording makes me choke up again, and I have to work hard to keep my voice strong.

"Hey, Dad, it's me, Kyle. Checking in like you said. Trying to check in. It's been impossible to get through. Everything here is okay. Uncle Matt . . . I've got that all under control. And, I heard from Mom. She's okay, too. They left the airport and are finding a hotel." I pause so I can manage this last part. "Call when you can. I know you probably can't, but Uncle Matt and me, we're seriously worried about you."

The boy opens the door.
    Kyle?
    He smiles, hopeful. "Yeah?"
Could I please get a glass of water?

I head to the kitchen for the water, but realize Uncle Matt is still in the bathroom. I need to get him first.

I'll get him cleaned up and settled, then tell him about the girl, then maybe make us all some food.

Shelves.
Bookcases.
Desk.
Chair.
Wings with fluttering white feathers.
I try to pinpoint myself here.
        In this apartment,
        in this room,
        in this bed.
            (Citrus trees in blue glazed pots,
                fruit falling like polka-dot rain.
            A rumble of thunder,
                loud enough to rattle things . . .)
I bolt upright and walk to the window
                (A cherrywood casket under a blue sky . . .)
A red velvet curtain comes down.

"Uncle Matt."

His head bobs up when I open the bathroom door.

This is the worst part, seeing him like this, wiping his ass. I do it fast, pull up his sweats, and hoist him back in his chair.

I wash my hands and his with a warm soapy washcloth, noticing the bottles on the counter.

"Hey, Uncle Matt, are you supposed to take any of these?" There must be ten different kinds of painkillers, anti-inflammatories, and muscle relaxants, but I know some of them have been here for months. I remember Mom saying one of the medications is to prevent clotting or something, so he doesn't get an embolism from sitting.

". . . Jus . . . four . . . Advih is . . . guh for . . . now."

There's a plastic cup on the sink with a straw. I help him take them and wheel him back to the living room.

The long-haired boys
  watch me.
    "Hanson. MMMBop," it reads above them.
I tap the bottle through the flannel,
  run my fingers along
    the feathery edge of the wings that hang
    from the back of the desk chair.
(Words slip in, echoing and distant:
    embôîté,
    attitude devant . . .)
I pull out the chair, and sit,
  (. . . *tombé* . . . *piques* . . .)
wait for them to pass.

"So, I have to tell you something," I say, once I have Uncle Matt situated in the living room. "You want the TV on?"

"Yeah. Buh . . . fay'ing . . . win-oh . . . kay?" It takes me a second to decipher: a request to turn him to see out the window. I reluctantly wheel him around to face the thick plumes of brown smoke that stream up over lower Manhattan.

A vacuuming sound comes from the back of his throat, his breath catching at the sight.

"Yeah, it's really bad," I say. "Way worse than it looks on the news. It felt like I was in some *Die Hard* movie or *Air Force One* when I was running across the bridge. Speaking of which," I add quietly, "on my way across, I saw something and, well, I didn't realize what it was. Not at first, but then I went back and, uh, I sort of found this girl."

He makes another noise, and his neck twitches as if he's trying to turn his head. But he can't, which, at this moment, is better for me. It's easier to talk if I don't have to look him in the face.

"I don't know who she is, or what she was doing, but there was no way to turn back. So I brought her here. She's, like, my age. I couldn't leave her there alone."

He doesn't say anything, so I babble the rest of the story rapid-fire, going back to this morning, Mrs. Bright's classroom, the first plane hitting. To how we thought it was something minor—a car backfiring, or maybe a gunshot, at worst. How, when we realized it was a plane, we still thought it was only an accident with a small plane.

"Until the second plane hit," I say, "and then we realized. We knew. In some of the other classrooms, the kids . . . they actually saw it fly in. And, after that, there was an announcement, and they sent us all back to homeroom, and we were evacuated. When the south tower went down, our whole freaking building shook."

It's weird to recap the story, staring at the aftermath out our window. At least I'm home safe. I hope safe. Homeroom seems like forever ago.

"I swear, Uncle Matt, I think they were worried the whole city was going to blow . . . Anyway, one of the teachers took us—the few of us from Brooklyn—to the bridge. Everyone else went uptown instead. But I lost everyone once we got on the bridge."

Uncle Matt sort of nods. Encouraged, I keep going. "When I reached the pillars, I thought I saw . . . something . . ." I leave out the wings, and thinking the girl was a bird, which seems dumb now. "And so I went back. And there she was, all crouched down. She was a mess and no one was helping her, so I brought her here . . ." I trail off, also leaving out that she didn't want to come, and how she was leaning out over the edge.

"She was covered in ash, Uncle Matt. I'm pretty sure she must have been *at* the towers. Anyway, she's in Kerri's room now, showered and resting. She seems okay, but I'm not sure what I should do with her. I guess I can take her down to the precinct on Gold Street."

"You . . . don . . . go . . . ou . . . yeh. You nee call . . . Mih-sing Per . . . suhs . . ." he says.

"I can try, but I won't get through."

"Try . . . la-yer."

"Okay," I say. "I will. Besides—" I pause for a minute, trying to figure out how to phrase this last part. "I'm not sure exactly what to tell them, Uncle Matt. I don't know her name. And she doesn't, either. I don't think she knows who she is."

In the desk drawer:
             pens, markers,
       hair ribbons.

A diary:

PROPERTY OF KERRI ANNE DONAHUE.

I touch the small plastic lock.

It doesn't require a real key.

I wait for Kyle to return with water,

    the bottle still squeezed in my hand.

I leave Uncle Matt in the living room and go to my room to lie down. I know I have shit to do, but I just need a minute to rest. I am suddenly completely wiped out. But when I try to close my eyes, they pop open again, a thousand worries bouncing in my brain.

I pull out my cell phone and hold it over my head. No new messages. But now I realize why I didn't hear calls coming in before. *Idiot.* My phone is still set on silent from school.

"Mr. Donohue, if a tree falls in the forest, but no one is there to hear it, does it make a sound?"

I rectify that, hoping more messages might come through, but they don't, so I toss it on my night table and grab my backpack, fishing out the small white paperback I shoved in there with all my other stuff this morning when we fled from Mrs. Bright's classroom.

Salinger's *Nine Stories.* We were discussing one of the stories when the first plane hit. Mrs. Bright says all of his stories are like Zen koans.

I thumb through pages, reading the titles to distract myself: "A Perfect Day for Bananafish." "Uncle Wiggly in Connecticut." "To Esme, With Love and Squalor." All the ones we've read so far are weird. The Bananafish one, for example, which takes place after World War II.

It's about this guy named Seymour who's on vacation in Florida with his wife. His wife is shallow and self-absorbed, only talking about her nails and clothes, all while Seymour is having some sort of nervous breakdown.

Before the story starts, Seymour has left the hotel room and gone out to the beach, where he meets this little girl named Sybil who creepily flirts with him. They go for a swim, and Seymour tells her how it's a perfect day to catch bananafish, which he says are a type of tragic fish because they eat bananas until they're too fat to swim out through the holes in the coral caves. So, they get stuck there, and starve and die.

Instead of the girl telling Seymour that there are no such things as bananafish, she says she's seen them, too. Then she leaves, and Seymour goes back to his hotel room and shoots himself in the head.

Mrs. Bright says the story is a metaphor about war and materialism, a Zen koan about people's inability to communicate.

I shut the book and sit up.

Here's a Zen koan: *If there's a girl down the hall and I ignore her, is it like I never met her and brought her home?*

FUGUE

I slip the diary out.

     Prying, but whatever.

None of it means anything to me.

Turn to the first page:

    IF YOU ARE NOT ME, DO NOT READ THIS.

Flip to the next:

    HEY, WHY ARE YOU READING?!?!!!

I can't help it and

    smile

                (. . . *promise me you'll smile, Papillon . . .*).

        Ms. Lansing says to set goals.

        Goal #1: By the time I turn 15,

        be a television star like Jennifer Aniston.

        On a hit TV show like Friends.

Her name is signed in curlicue script underneath:

           Kerri Anne Donohue.

The dot over the *i* is a heart.

The washer has stopped again. I pull out the girl's stuff, hold her shirt to my nose, and inhale deeply. *Much better.* Nothing but fresh, soapy clean.

Shit. I never brought her the glass of water.

Then again, I guess she could've walked to the kitchen herself.

The diary falls open,

        a photograph wedged in its center:

The boy, Kyle, with

      a young girl.

      Her face is his, but with freckles,

           her hair way redder than his.

They're in front of a waterfall.

The girl is nine or ten,

    in a pink bikini top and denim cutoffs.

She sits on his shoulders.

He's laughing.

Her hands are covering his eyes.

BASH BISH FALLS, July 2000,

she's written,

BEST BROTHER IN. THE. WORLD.

I shut the book,

close my eyes.

The shadows creep in.

My eyes shift to the top of the dryer where her bra is. I reach out and run my finger along the still-damp edge.

None of your business, asshole.

I turn the dryer on, then flip the tag anyway and squint at the faded label.

CALVIN KLEIN BARE. 32B.

I walk toward the stage again,

to where the burgundy curtain hangs.

Heavy,

as if in a trance.

As if sleepwalking.

I bring a glass of water to Kerri's room. But when I knock and open the door, the girl is sleeping, so I leave it on the desk and head back to the kitchen to make lunch. I'm not hungry, but we need to eat.

I put three mini frozen pizzas in the toaster oven, set the timer, and sit at the table, willing the phone to ring.

It doesn't. The only sounds in our apartment are the drone of the television and the quiet *click, click, click* of the toaster marking down time.

From the living room, I hear a reporter say that U.S. airspace is clear of all flights going in and out of the country. And that a bomb threat has shut down LAX.

Why hasn't Mom called again?

I go back to my room and pick up the Salinger book, but I'm way too distracted to read. Instead, I turn on my computer. When it boots up, I open the web browser and type *amnesia* into a search engine.

Anterograde.

Retrograde.

Transient.

Turns out, there is no shortage of types of amnesia.

Hysterical or "fugue," that last one in quotes. *"Fugue."*

Fugue amnesia is a rare phenomenon wherein patients forget not only their past, but their very identity. A person could wake up and suddenly not have any sense at all of who they are—even if they look in the mirror, they do not recognize their own reflection. The details in their wallet—driver's license, credit cards, IDs—are all meaningless to a person experiencing a fugue state.

I scroll down to the part labeled *triggers*:

This type of amnesia is usually triggered by an event that the person's mind is unable to cope with properly. In most cases the memory either slowly or suddenly comes back within a few days, although the memory of the trigger event may never return completely.

I glance at my clock. It's almost one, and I still haven't heard back from Dad. In the kitchen, the timer goes off.

The curtain lifts and music plays,
    faint at first
        then swelling,
           louder and louder.
On stage,
    the lake shimmers.
        Cattails and swamp grasses grow tall and wild all
around.
As I move closer, the music grows sharper:
        Danse de fançailles.
        Allegro, tempo guisto.
You appear on that far shore.
        and I press through the muck-matted grasses
           to get to you.
    But my boots sink in,
  weighted and sticking,
    so that my legs can't move forward,
      and the shore where you stand
      recedes farther
        and farther
          away.
I cup my hand to my eyes,

squint to try to see you,
but an alarm sounds,
        and the air fills with the smell
of
            burnt things.

The pizza is black.

I set it on broil instead of bake.

I chuck it in the garbage, put three new pieces in, and try Dad's cell phone to no avail. Then I stare at the phone, telepathically willing Mom to call. To let me know they made it out of LAX.

Tired of that, I go back to the bathroom. The dryer has a minute left, so I sit on the toilet and wait.

I hear it again: something clinking inside its drum. A definite pinging sound. I open the door and reach in, pull out the girl's things, shaking and folding each piece. Shirt, pants, sweatshirt, underwear.

I unfold the underwear and slip them beneath the pants with her bra, my ears growing warm just touching them.

With everything out, I feel around inside the drum and quickly find the source of the noise: a small key chain in the corner. Not a key chain, exactly, but a clear plastic card sleeve tied to pink ribbon, knotted to a small enamel charm. The charm is shaped like a ballet slipper. The toe shoe kind with the crisscross ribbons that go up the leg, like my sister is learning how to use.

The card sleeve looks like what you might keep a monthly train ticket in, or a photo ID. I keep my school ID in my wallet, but some of the kids at Stuyvesant wear theirs like that, tied around their necks or to their backpacks. I search for more loose things in the dryer but come up empty-handed.

I shake her pants from the top of the pile and feel around, thinking maybe something is still in one of the many pockets, but I don't find anything there, either.

I slip the sleeve with the charm into my pocket, refold the pants, and walk to Kerri's room, leaving the pile of clothes next to her boots.

Confused,
    I sit up.
My eyes dart about the room.
Brooklyn Heights.
The boy.
The bridge.
Before that?
       Nothing.
       Edges that fade into
            blackness.
But wait:
     On the desk, a glass of water.
     He must have left it there for me.
I drink it down fast
trying to quench my endless thirst,
    then stop,
remembering now,
and saving the last few sips for
     the pills.

The timer *ding*s, and I fork out the three pizzas, cutting Uncle Matt's into fish food–sized bites. Setting his aside to cool, I put the girl's piece on a plate and carry it to Kerri's room.

Shake the pills into my palm:

        not a lot, but enough.

My gaze shifts to the window,

      to the desk and the drawer

         with the diary.

      BEST BROTHER IN. THE. WORLD.

I take a deep breath,

bring my hand to my mouth

glancing once more at the plaid pajama pants,

    the blue T-shirt,

    with the yellow planet on the front.

The boy has been nice,

trying,

      but I can't—

      Everything feels too precarious.

One wrong move,

      and the eye floaters will rush in like a deluge.

I'm the dork in the middle of a disaster, listening at my sister's door with a plate of toaster pizza in my hand. Her pile of clothes sits untouched next to the boots.

No noise inside, so I guess she's still asleep.

In the living room, the news drones on about more bomb threats, and a third building that's gone down somewhere near the Twin Towers. About the president being moved to a bunker, about more hits that might be coming soon. About the rising number of estimated dead.

And, suddenly, I'm glad the girl is here. Someone else, at least, who can walk and talk and hang out with me, while I wait for the phone to ring.

I knock gently. No answer.

Screw it. The pizza will get cold.

I knock again, and open the door.

NOT A PLANET

The girl lies facedown, dead to the world.

Whatever has happened to her, I'm not waking her for a stupid piece of pizza.

I walk out, gently closing the door.

Maybe when she gets up, she'll remember everything. We'll figure out, then, how to get her home.

The door opens and
            closes.
I sit up,
        open my fist,
                stare at the sweaty pills stuck to my palm.
I scrape them back into the bottle,
            glancing down again at the shirt he gave me,
                    at the yellow planet.
    The planet is not a planet but a lemon.
                Bright and happy-faced,
                smiling up at me
                like a
                promise.

ACT OF TERROR

Dad doesn't call, yet another building near the tower goes down, and, as far as I know, the girl sleeps through the rest of the afternoon. Uncle Matt, too, finally dozes off in his chair.

I sit on the couch and stare at the TV. They say the president is calling it an act of terror.

I tell myself Mom is off at some hotel and can't get through in the chaos, and Dad is okay, too, just too busy rescuing people. He'll call me as soon as he can. I tell myself over and over, but I'm having a hard time believing it. If he were okay, wouldn't he have checked in by now?

Then again, the reporter had said something about the cell towers there being down. Still, it's hard not to let my brain run away with fear, not to imagine him dead and buried beneath the burning rubble of the buildings.

The news repeats itself; everyone's waiting on new information. The stations replay the planes hitting, the wall of smoke, and speculate as to the groups in the Middle East, whose names I've never heard of, that might be responsible. Some terrorism expert comes on and says we should fear more hits, be prepared, stay inside. A senator comes on to say he suspects the mastermind is someone named Osama bin Laden.

I've never heard of him, but I bet Dad has.

A new clip now airs of President Bush being told of the attacks, a secret service guy leaning down to whisper to him while he reads a picture book in a classroom to a group of kids.

The president nods, and his face shifts, changes for a split second, but then he goes back to reading to the kids. After another minute he gets up and leaves the room, impressively calm.

Yet another clip plays of the president announcing that U.S. military forces are on "high alert." In this one he seems more nervous, and his eyes are filled with tears.

I switch off the television and head back to my room just as the girl is walking out of my parents' room.

"Hey," I try not to let on that she startled me.

"I had to go to the bathroom," she says. Her eyes dart away as if she's embarrassed.

"No problem," I say, but I can't help wonder why she didn't use my bathroom, the same one she showered in earlier.

"And I'm really sorry about all this," she adds, but keeps walking past me back to Kerri's room.

I follow her. "Sorry about what?"

"Me, here, like this."

"Don't be. I'm sorry about the accommodations." I gesture around Kerri's room, at the cheesy bedspread and purple walls, at the Hanson poster that hangs there like a blister. "Besides, I'm the one who brought you here." She looks to where I nod, so I say, "*That* is not my taste, by the way, I swear."

She cracks a smile, so I add, "My little sister was obsessed with them for a while. Now it's *NSYNC. She has no taste in music at all. She's all about boy bands and Radio Disney, anything lame and pop. Probably because she thinks one day she's going to be the star of her own Nickelodeon show."

The girl smiles again. "How old is she?"

"Twelve."

"Where is she now?"

"In LA, with my mom. Long story. But the short version is that they've been gone all summer. They were supposed to come home today, but with the—" I stop. It's the first normal conversation we're having, and I don't want to say anything that might set her off or trigger something. If she was down there, and is traumatized, and now can't remember anything, there may be a good reason.

"Anyway," I say instead, "it turns out they're not coming home for a day or two, maybe more, so it's okay for now if you stay here. I don't mind the company. Really."

I look back at the wall, at the dreaded Hanson brothers on the piss-yellow background.

"Thanks," she says, looking there too. "'MMMBop'. Hanson. Yeah, I think I remember them."

DINNER

Dinner is weird.

Then again, everything else is, so why shouldn't dinner be?

For starters, I'm the one who makes it.

I've watched my dad whip up pasta enough times to know mostly what to do, so I boil water and pull some fresh ravioli and a container of Dad's sauce from the freezer, trying to remember what else he adds in.

It feels strange to be doing normal things like cooking with the city a mess, the world a mess, and my dad still out there somewhere in the middle of all of it. But Dad would tell me to. He'd be glad I was making us dinner.

Dad is the cook in our house. His father—my grandfather—was Irish, but my grandmother, Anna, was 100 percent Italiana. An "off-the-boat" Sicilian. She taught all three of her boys to cook "the Sicilian way," which means Dad only buys homemade pasta from Messina's or Savino's or a few other places in Williamsburg. Every couple of months, he makes sauce from scratch from stewed tomatoes, garlic, and basil, which he portions out and keeps in meal-sized containers in the freezer.

I defrost one in the microwave, cut up a few cloves of fresh garlic, and put that in a pan with some olive oil. When the garlic sizzles and the sauce is loose, I drop a bay leaf in, and turn the heat down and let it all simmer. That's about as good as it gets considering I never cook.

When the ravioli is done, I drain it and pour it into a bowl with the sauce over it. I leave a hunk of Parmesan on the table with the small hand grater in the center, wheel Uncle Matt in, and go to get the girl. But when I reach Kerri's room, she's not there.

For a second I panic. *Maybe she left.* But then the bathroom door opens and she comes out looking normal, eyebrows raised questioningly at me.

She's dressed in her own clothes, my PopMart Tour T-shirt and pajama pants folded neatly in her hands.

"I'll put these on your sister's bed," she says.

"Are you going somewhere?" I sound too alarmed, desperate. But I can't help it; I don't want her to get hurt, wandering out there alone. Not to mention, I don't want to be left here, with just Uncle Matt, in this disaster.

"I should, right?"

"No! I mean, where would you go? It's getting late, and it's not safe out there. Even my dad said—" I break off. All I can think of is her going back out there, on the bridge. With the city—no, the whole country—under attack. "You need to stay. I really want you to stay. There's a hospital a few blocks away, and a police precinct. Have some dinner, and I'll ask my uncle what we should do. He's a cop, too, like my dad. I mean, not now he isn't—not anymore—well, you'll see. But I can bring you there after, or tomorrow. Tomorrow is better. Better to go when it's light out."

She looks away, unsure.

"Please stay," I say again. "You can't go out there, not knowing."

I sit next to Uncle Matt where Dad usually does, so I can cut up his ravioli into pathetic little mashed-up pieces. The girl sits on his other side, where I normally sit.

"This is my uncle, Matt," I say, "And this, Uncle Matt, is . . ." *Who? The girl with the wings? The suicidal amnesiac bird girl?* "This is the girl I told you about."

Uncle Matt's head bobs up toward her with effort, and she smiles. Not with pity, though, the way most people who know him do, gawking like my friends when they finally see him post-accident, no matter how much I try to prepare them.

He grunts his half-formed "Hello," and lets his head loll back to the side.

"Uncle Matt was a lieutenant in the NYPD, like my dad, but in a different unit. He broke his neck and jaw," I explain, "and fractured his skull, in an accident this past summer. The wires in his mouth just came out a few weeks ago. There's still a plate in there, though. Over here." I pat the side of my cheek at the jawline. "So it's going to take a while before he can talk well again. But the doctors say the swelling is still coming down, and he could improve a lot. And he is getting better, right, Uncle Matt?" I don't wait for an answer. "Come on, now, eat."

I take his hand and move it forward to close it around his fork, then stab up a speck of pasta and move it to his mouth. He opens weakly, like a baby bird, and lets me slip it in.

"I'm doing all the work." I frown. "You know you're supposed to do it for me. Like Karina says. Oh, and no comment about the food. I already know it's not as good as Dad's."

Six months ago, Uncle Matt would have laughed at that, but now he just makes a lame gurgling noise.

I get up, pour ice water into each of our glasses, slip a plastic straw in his, and hold it to his lips. He sips, a small bit dribbling down the side of his chin. I look over at the girl, who's pushing her food around with a fork.

"Not good? My dad is the chef around here."

She forks up a bite. "No, no, it is. Really. It's—" She doesn't finish, because Uncle Matt interrupts, blurting something that sounds like gibberish.

"Ace . . . cubs . . . bah door! Op-eh . . . Sev-uh spays . . . guh . . . in . . . han . . . Ace . . . wife . . . Four hars . . ." It's not the first time he's done this. Lately, it's like he has Tourette's. He nods at me—and keeps going. "Four hars . . . run . . . kitch-eh . . . too lay . . ."

My eyes dart to the girl, slightly embarrassed. He started doing it a few days ago. Like some new brain neurons are firing, and he doesn't quite have control over them. It sounds like a sense-less jumble, but it's not. I know exactly what he's doing—saying. It's a good sign, actually. A really good sign.

He's reciting cards with their suits as if they are people, as-signing them actions. "Ace of Clubs at the back door. Opens it for the Seven of Spades." That kind of thing. It's a practiced skill called the method of loci, a memory trick in which certain types of data get stored in storylike sequences. Then the actions get deconstructed, re-broken down, back to their original form. In this case, to remember a basic deck of cards.

It's downright smart what he's doing. Brilliant, even. Because he hasn't held a deck of cards in months. So, he must be remem-bering some deck he knew back then. Before his accident.

Still, my cheeks turn hot, and I feel bad for him. They sound like the ramblings of a crazy man.

The man Kyle calls Uncle Matt mumbles,
    clubs,
        hearts,
            more.
    Words that sound like suits in a
    deck of cards.
Kyle looks at me,
    apologetic.
But I like Uncle Matt and his garbled words.
    They sound like the thoughts inside my head.

Uncle Matt is a genius and a memory expert. He has an IQ of 152. Only eight points lower than Einstein's. I never got why he wasted it being a cop. I know that sounds wrong, but he could have cured cancer, or run for president, or been the next Bill Gates or something. I asked him about it once, and he said, "It's easy to be smart if you're born that way, Kyle. It's infinitely harder to be brave."

Maybe he's right. Maybe smart is easy and brave is hard.

And, he hasn't said this, but I know he must want to be out there with Dad and Uncle Paul. Being brave. Saving people. Doing his job. But I bet he misses the other part of his life, too. The memory competition stuff. Before the accident, he was planning to go to the U.S. Memory Championship for his third time. And he was planning to win it this time.

My eyes shift back to his plate, the small, uneaten pieces of pasta making me sick to my stomach. "Eat, Uncle Matt!" I say, too forcefully. "You're starting to waste away." I fork up a piece myself and move it to his mouth. "You have to eat and get stronger."

Uncle Matt's eyes move away, and he chews. When he's finished, he mumbles, "Three . . . hars . . . bal-co-y . . . fi-uhs shahs . . . King . . . dia-onds. No. Sick . . . cubs."

I glance sideways at the girl to see if she's weirded out, but she's smiling as she picks at her food.

(Glazed blue pots.

Flames . . .

Fruitfallingfromtrees . . .

Embôîté attitude

Devant).

A jumble of words, images,

voices

half there, half not.
>Floating,
>>disjointed,
>>disappearing.
Like the uncle's words,
>I watch them go by,
>>pop up,
>>disperse like
>>dandelion seeds.
>>>(. . . "Smile, *Papillon*!")
Coming and going of their own volition.

"It means something," I finally say to the girl, feeling defensive. "The stuff that my uncle is saying."

"I know," she says. "I can tell. It sounds like playing cards or something?"

I'm surprised, and a little impressed. It's like she's somehow in tune with him.

I explain the method of loci, and find myself proudly telling her how Uncle Matt came in seventh at the US Memory Championship last year, sixteenth the year before. "This year, we seriously thought he could win. At least place top three, and a decent cash prize comes with that." I catch her look, which is sympathetic, like she completely cares about every stupid thing I'm saying. "But that was before the SUV," I say. "I used to help him train. The competition was in Boston this year. I was supposed to go with him."

"What happened?"

"He was on his motorcycle on the BQE, after a date. The other guy—the one in the SUV—fell asleep. And, no, my uncle wasn't drinking. Everyone asks that." I always add that last part, because it's the first thing people assume when they hear what happened. "He nearly died, broke his spine . . ." I look at Uncle Matt and stop. He doesn't need to hear the ugly replay. The spinal cord injury. The swelling on his brain. The surgeries to try to repair things. Besides, she can probably figure it out by the mumbling and drooling and itty-bitty pasta pieces. By his ragdoll neck and dead-fish right hand. Which is the one that works at all.

She looks up, first at me, then over at Uncle Matt, who rolls his head up and says, "Ky-uh . . . where . . . you . . . dah?"

"I know," I say, trying not to break down and cry. "It's getting late. I wish we'd hear from him."

"I'm sorry about your accident. That sucks," the girl says, which for some reason makes me smile.

I relax a little, and we eat some more in silence, until the phone miraculously rings.

I give them privacy,
head back to the sister's room.
Sit,
blank and restless.
          With people but
                totally
alone.

Lie down, try to sleep, but
      the lake shimmers,
             and shadowy things
                   dart like tadpoles through murky water.

(I wait and I wait, but
you don't
return.)

I race to the phone, but no one is there when I answer.

I try Dad's cell phone, but it rings through to voicemail.

I focus on Uncle Matt while Dad's voice plays: "You've reached Detective Tom Donohue. Please leave your name, number, and reason for your call. If this is a true emergency, please hang up and dial 911."

"Hey, Dad, it's Kyle." I try not to get choked up, not to sound like a baby. If he's okay, he needs me in control here. I load the last of our dinner dishes into the dishwasher, then turn on the faucet to rinse the large pasta pot. "No worries here. Everything is okay. But we haven't heard from you. And we just want to know that you're all right."

I hang up and wheel Uncle Matt to the living room for more news. The never-ending crawl at the bottom of the TV informs that the dead and missing number in the thousands.

It also reports a fourth building has gone down.

"Countless rescue workers are unaccounted for," it reads.

I drift off.

    The lake is gone.

    The curtain lifts on a

        white room.

    Small and bare,

        only a bed, a window,

        and one buzzing florescent.

Pink peonies in vases line the sill.

I sit in a chair.

The boy stands, watches me from the door.

An orderly appears,

holds up a calloused finger,

then whistles while he sweeps silky, black strands

from the floor.

Finished,

he rests the broom against the wall,

looks up, and says,

"You can go now."

At eight P.M. the phone rings again. I run to the kitchen, heart pounding, and pray.

It's Mom, which is almost as good. I mean, good, but bad, too. Because what am I going to tell her about Dad?

She sounds worried and drained. "Hundreds of people in a small radius all looking for hotels," she says. "And no phone calls getting through to New York. You won't believe the fiasco."

I would, I want to say. *I do.*

She tells me LAX was evacuated, which I know, and that even in LA there are bomb threats.

"I finally called Kerri's acting teacher," she says, "the one who ran the camp. She's very kind. So, for now, we're staying with her."

"That's good," I say, dreading the next question.

"So, did you speak to your father? I can't get anything but his message thing." Her voice is hopeful, expectant. Like she's assuming I have.

"No," I whisper. "Not yet. But he did leave me a message this morning. He said it was hard to make calls. So I'm sure he'll get in touch, Mom. When he can. He's probably so busy in there, helping. And the cell towers," I add, remembering. "They went down, too . . ."

"Jesus, Kyle . . ." A sob escapes, and she blows her nose.

"I know. But you know Dad. He'll be fine. I'm sure of it." I try to sound like I believe it.

"I know, Kyle, thank you. Me, too, honey," she whispers. "I just wish I could hear his voice . . ." She starts to say something else, to give me the name and number of the place where she's staying, but I can't hear—can't think—because the call-waiting is beeping.

"Hold on, Mom! Shoot! Wait, never mind! Call me right back!" I hang up to let the other call through.

I can't miss it. Caller ID shows that it's Dad.

Air.

    Water.

  Wings.

    Bone.

      (How can you be gone?)

I freeze. I can't get words out, because another thought hits me: what if it's not Dad calling? What if it's someone else calling us from his phone? Because he can't, so they have to. And they're using his phone to give us the bad news.

"Ky-uh . . . who . . . is . . . ih?" Uncle Matt asks, snapping me out of it. I breathe deeply, and croak out a hello.

"Hey, son, is everything all right?"

I double over with relief. I could cry. Okay, *shit*. Maybe I do start to cry.

He's alive. He's okay.

"Kyle, you there?"

He sounds hoarse, beyond tired. He sounds awful, but I don't care. I'm so damn happy he's alive.

"Yeah, I'm here," I say, "you okay?"

There's so much noise in the background, it's hard to hear what he says, something that ends with, "And, you?" I clear my throat.

"We're fine, Dad. I tried to reach you. I left messages . . . I was just on the phone with Mom. She's really worried about you . . ."

"I know, Kyle. I got your message this morning, knew you made it home safe and were with Matty. Listen, there's no service down here. Nothing . . ." When he speaks again, his voice breaks completely, which is hard to take. "Can you call her for me? Tell her I love her. And let her know I'm all right."

"Yeah, of course I will," I say, trying not to lose it now myself. "She's calling me back any minute. They're staying with Kerri's acting teacher from the camp. And Uncle Matt is good. I'm taking care of everything here."

"I know you are, son. I'm not likely getting calls down here any time soon. It's total chaos. I can barely . . ." His voice breaks again, then disappears. When it returns, it's more measured. "Our guys are down here, too, Kyle, under everything . . . I have to—you understand? I have to stay and get them out. The whole unit will stay down here . . . I don't know how long. I'm going to need you to manage without me for a while more."

"Yeah," I say. "It's fine. We're fine . . . I'll tell Mom."

A fresh round of banging and machinery starts up in the background. "Okay, I've got to go, kid. Give Matty a kiss for me. I'm proud of you." He stops. No, not stops. My badass dad is crying. I wait for his regular voice to return again, normal, safer sounding. But instead he says, "And stay inside, you hear me? Don't go anywhere. Not until we know for sure what's going on."

"Okay. I promise," I say. And, though I know I shouldn't, I ask, "Are you sure you're going to be all right?"

"I hope so, kid. I think so. The military is all over it now. But I don't know when I'll be home. Not tonight. So hold down the fort."

"Okay, we will." My eyes dart down the hall. *Me, Uncle Matt, and the bird girl.* "Do what you need to do," I say. "I'll let Mom know now."

He hangs up. I let out a shaky breath and wait for my mother to call back.

WAR ZONES

At midnight I call Marcus. He's probably sound asleep, but our apartment is too quiet, and calls finally seem to be going through.

I shouldn't be awake, either. I'm tired, and the girl has been asleep for hours. And it took a whole lot of effort to get Uncle Matt ready for bed.

Still, I'm restless and figure I might as well bother him, do something that feels normal for a minute.

His phone rings four times before he picks up. "Shit, mon, what the fock?"

"Hey, sorry, dude. Didn't mean to wake you, just thought I'd check in."

"Is after midnight, no?"

Marcus is from Uganda, and if you catch him off guard before he checks himself, his otherwise faded accent is especially strong. Sharp on the *T*'s and hard consonants, soft on *R*'s, drawn out on some vowels, long on others. Bangor and the other guys joke that he's Rastafarian or Jamaican, and Bangor calls him *Sanka Coffie* after the guy from the movie *Cool Runnings*, which is moronic since we repeatedly tell him that Uganda has nothing to do with Jamaica. Obviously, geography isn't Bangor's strong suit, and Marcus thinks it's funny.

Marcus has a good sense of humor, which is amazing, since his early life was horrible in a way he doesn't like to talk about. We give him shit sometimes about how weird he is, forgetting how bad it really was. I think his real parents were murdered in a refugee camp, but I don't know the whole story. All I know is that he was adopted from there when he was five or six. "Adopted, possibly," he likes to joke, "into the whitest family in all of America." His dad is Scandinavian—pale skin, white-blond hair and eyebrows. His mom is pale, too—Irish, with bright red hair that makes mine look blond and even my sister's look washed out.

He calls his parents here Mom and Dad, and never talks about what happened to his real family in Uganda. "This *is* my real family," he once said when I asked. "The others, bock there, they but a dream. Like the song about the rowboat, you know?"

I never really pushed him again.

His parents here are awesome, rich but super laid back. Since he had such a hard life before, I think all they want for him now is to be happy. They spoil him ridiculously, and support everything he does. The way my dad always does with Kerri. But not me.

Kerri's a girl. What are you going to do with all that music? The Donohue men share a tradition . . .

"You there, mon?" Marcus asks, bringing me back. "You call me, remember?"

"Yeah, sorry. It's been crazy here, dude. My dad is still down there, you know?"

"Oh, fock, Kyle, I didn't think about that."

"It's okay. I couldn't reach him all day, but he called a few hours ago . . . I swear, Marcus, I was sure . . ." I don't finish the thought. "Anyway, he's all right now, but he's Task Force, you know? So I don't know when he'll be home."

"Whoa, that's crazy."

"I know, right?" It's quiet, then I add, "By the way, it wasn't *after* midnight when I called. It was *exactly* midnight. I looked at a clock."

Marcus laughs. It's so good to hear him laugh. To hear anyone laugh.

"Whatever, mon," he says, "Is not like we have school in the morning."

"Yeah, that's what I was thinking." This fact settles over us. It could be days—weeks—before we go back again. "Any idea when?" I ask.

"No, you?"

"No." There's another pause, and you can tell we're both thinking about this morning, watching the first tower go down, the chaos that followed in the hallways when they announced they were evacuating all of Lower Manhattan. "So, is the city weird?"

"Understatement. You're lucky you in Brooklyn. No one outside here and, of course, my parents be flippin'. No subways running. No restaurants open. It's like the focking zombie apocalypse."

"I hear you," I say, smiling a little because Marcus's cursing sounds nice, like music or something. He can get away with it, even in front of my dad. But when he speaks again, his voice is so quiet I can barely hear it.

"Like a focking war zone," he says.

And then I get choked up because I can tell it's all making him think about home—about Uganda and whatever fucked-up shit happened there, about losing his parents—and today, for once, I understand that better than I ever really understood it before.

It's not like I know much about his country's history, only the stuff we've learned in social studies about Idi Amin and the guys who came after him whose names I can't remember. How, for decades, there was a constant state of genocide. Maybe there still is. Jesus, I should know more about it. I'm going to make a point to learn more.

"I know," I say, "Here, too, but probably not as bad as in the city. But—get this, dude—not only is my dad down there, but my mom and Kerri were supposed to be flying home today . . ."

I hear Marcus sit up in his bed. When he talks again, he sounds clearer, more sharp.

"Holy shit, Kyle. They still in California?"

"Yeah. Remember I told you Kerri got that callback thing?

Well, they had that yesterday and were supposed to fly back this morning. They could have been on one of those planes."

"Shit," he says, again. "Sorry, man. I didn't realize."

"Yeah, I know. But so far everyone's okay." For the first time all day, I feel better about things, talking to Marcus about all of this crap. Like there's a good reason I've been so freaked out all day, like I'm not some big wuss, because it's actually a big deal that I've been alone in this mess, waiting to hear from everyone. "It's been surreal, dude," I say. "And I have to take care of Uncle Matt . . ."

I trail off when I hear the bathroom door open and close down the hall. The girl must be up. I still haven't told Marcus about her. I don't want to. I think maybe I'm worried he'll think I'm crazy for bringing her here, or maybe he won't believe me. Maybe I don't completely believe it myself.

"Anyway, I should let you get back to sleep."

"Yeah, okay," he says. "But now that I'm up, I should tell you . . ." His voice trails off, and when he speaks again, it's different, more serious, making my stomach lurch. "You hear about Bangor? And Jenny's dad?"

Bangor's real name is Alex Barton. We call him Bangor because he's from a small town in Maine called that, which you've got to admit is a pretty dumb name for a town. And Jenny Lynch is Kristen Coletti's best friend. Jenny's not exactly one of my favorite people, but Kristen is. She's one of my best friends. She and I dated for a while at the beginning of freshman year, just kid stuff, holding hands and going to movies. We all hang out a lot—Bangor, me, Marcus, Kristen, and Jenny.

"Shit, no," I say, wracking my brain in a panic to think whether I saw Bangor this morning.

"Bangor's uncle and Jenny's dad were both up there. In the towers. You talk to Kristen?"

"No," I say, reeling. "The news said not to call . . . I haven't tried anyone. Only my parents and you. I couldn't really reach anyone before . . ." I feel sick, awful, though relieved that Bangor is okay. "When did you talk to her?"

"I didn't. Bangor, he called me. Do you remember how he wasn't in homeroom? Turns out he was coming in late, not surprising, you know? Anyway, he was walking up Chambers when . . . He *saw* the whole focking thing, Kyle. The plane hitting, the explosion, people falling from the windows . . . He said he couldn't look. He turned and ran. Said paper and metal and things were falling through the sky like at a focking ticker-tape parade."

"Jesus." I think of the girl when I found her, bits of shiny things in her hair. I don't know what to say.

"Anyway, Bangor says his uncle was up there. And they haven't heard from him. And he told me Jenny's dad was up there, too. They work for the same big company, up on the hundred and fifth floor. He doesn't know if . . . Well, clearly, they aren't going to be . . . I mean, not likely, mon. Not at all."

"Jesus," I repeat, everything whirling. I try to steady my thoughts, double check in my brain that I talked to my dad. That I didn't imagine it. There are so many people dead. Everything feels uncertain now.

"You talk to her, Marcus?"

"To Jenny, no. But I'll call her tomorrow. You should, too."

"Yeah." I say. "Yeah."

I listen for the girl's footsteps in the hall. I think for a second that, if I can't hear her, maybe I can chalk this all up to a dream. More like a nightmare. A nightmare within a nightmare within a nightmare. "Yeah, I will," I say, anxious to hang up. I want to get up and go look for her. Make sure she's real. "Marcus?"

"Yeah."

"What are you going to say to her when you call?"

"No clue, Kyle. No focking clue."

I sit in the glare of the bathroom fixture
      shaking off
         ghosts.
    When I feel better, I stand and
      look in the mirror,
          then shut the lights
Leave her in the dark again.

I finally hang up with Marcus, but I don't hear the girl come back out.

There are probably still razor blades in there . . .

I pad quickly down the hall. Kerri's door is half open, but I can't see in from this angle. Down the hall, the bathroom door is open, lights off. So that's a good sign, at least.

I stop at Uncle Matt's door, the stuff Marcus told me about Bangor and Jenny circulating in my head. He's sleeping soundly, his atrophied self barely more than a slight, blanketed hump in the dark. Three months ago, Uncle Matt was living the life up on 103rd Street. Skiing, and running, and riding his motorcycle. Three months ago, he was a lieutenant dating beautiful women, having sex like a rock star, and on his way to being the memory champion of the U.S. Now, he could die in his sleep. Now, he sits in a wheelchair all day and drools. His life changed forever in one stupid second.

And Bangor's uncle is probably dead. Jenny's dad, too. Thousands of people, the reporter had said. How can that be true? How can a person get up and go to school on a Tuesday morning, their life all normal and fine and, then, a few minutes later, someone they love is dead? How can people be here, then, *boom,* gone? Life should be more permanent than that.

I pull Uncle Matt's door closed so I don't wake him, and head back to my room, slowing past Kerri's half open door to glance in.

My sister's bed is empty.

The girl isn't there.

Late Tuesday Night Into Early Wednesday Morning, 9.12.01

BITS AND PIECES

99 . . . 98 . . . 97
I count backward and
            think about leaving.
            As soon as the sun starts to rise.
But where will I go?
                        (. . . who will take care of me . . . ?)
Across the inky river,
            a sea of haloed lights twinkle through
            the dark, smoky haze.

A door opens.

I hear Kyle in the hall.

The girl stands with her back to me, face pressed to the living room window.

It's odd to see her there like that, some stranger in my clothes, in my apartment, in the middle of the night. But it's comforting, too. I'm happy she's here. Happy she's safe. It's something to keep my mind off those who aren't, off Bangor's uncle, off Jenny Lynch's dad.

Something to keep me from worrying about my dad.

I clear my throat, and she turns. From the back, with her short-cropped hair, she had looked almost boyish, but from the front she looks so sweet. Small and lost in my oversized T-shirt and pajama pants.

"Couldn't sleep?" I shift uncomfortably, then walk into the room to find the remote and switch on the TV, changing channels fast past the networks, the buildings and smoke and planes crashing down. With any luck, some regular programming will be back on cable. Maybe something good on Cartoon Network or Comedy Central. I could use something funny.

"No, I guess not."

"You okay?"

"I think so," she says. "Thanks."

"You sure?" I flip through channels. "Did you need something?"

Yes, Kyle, she should answer. *Obviously, I need something. I need many things. I need to go home. But first I need to know where home is. And it would be good to know my name, and not be here, in some dork guy's apartment, being asked stupid questions*

I can't answer. But she doesn't say any of that, just turns and looks out the window again.

On Cartoon Network, the end of an infomercial is on. I switch on the reading lamp behind the couch to its dimmest setting. The infomercial is for some high-tech vacuum. "Dust and mites," it says, "rubbed-in dirt and ash will disappear!" My mind flashes to yesterday morning, to the girl covered in ash, in those wings. To her black-ringed eyes, and her chopped hair. To her standing there at Kerri's open window.

Here, she looks so normal.

Pretty.

Beautiful.

A breaking-news flash comes on, interrupting the vacuum infomercial. A reporter interviewing a fireman in the dark. The floodlights around him bathe a scene of total destruction, as if it were a movie set. It's impossible to believe it's taking place right now across the river in Manhattan, or to imagine my dad is there.

I scan for him as the camera pans and the news crawl says rescue workers have been operating through the night, and that they've pulled two live bodies from the rubble. A video plays of a man walking with a German shepherd over piles of concrete and steel. I search for any sign of Dad in the dust-coated faces and uniforms, but I don't spot him. At any rate, I'm glad the girl isn't watching the screen.

Thankfully, the image changes back to the logo for Cartoon Network and titles start up for *Cow and Chicken.*

Cow and Chicken! Manna from heaven. I could seriously kiss the screen.

I sit on the couch and turn the volume up. It's the episode where Cow and Chicken mess with a copy machine and accidentally make an evil version of Chicken, who proceeds to wreak havoc on everything.

"It's weird, Kyle," the girl says, turning at the sound and taking a few steps closer to me. I lower the volume. Seeing her bathed in the blue glow of the television, I could convince myself all over again she's merely a figment of my overtired imagination.

"I keep remembering little things. Bits and pieces. Like those things that flash at the end of a movie reel when the film runs out. You know what I'm talking about? What do they call those again?"

"No idea," I say, "but I get what you're saying."

"Thanks." She raises her eyebrows, as if to ask if I'm humoring her. But I'm not. I do get it, at least sort of. "Anyway, it's like that. Like, I get an image or a voice in my head, but it's a blur, like I'm watching scenery rush past out a train window."

"Which pieces?" I ask, but maybe I'm missing the point. It's just that there's a lot I want to ask her—about today, about this morning, about now. About before all of that, and what she remembers and doesn't. About what she was doing down there at the towers, and about what she was trying to do on the bridge.

"I don't know, exactly," she says. "Voices. Faces. I keep having nightmares, so it's hard to tell if any of it is real." She closes her eyes and shakes her head, then points her toes and slides her foot in a small arc across the carpet. "And music and dance steps," she says, making the motion again.

The pink ribbon with the enamel toe shoe charm flashes in my head. I should tell her. But she seems fragile, so maybe I should wait. She continues so softly that I'm mesmerized by her and forget the key chain, and *Cow and Chicken*, and everything except the way she moves and the sound of her voice, lost in the way her head tilts when she's trying to think of something, in the way her jagged hair frames her sad, wide-eyed face.

"What about your name?" I finally ask.

She shrugs.

"Your family? Anything?"

She shakes her head, and neither of us says anything after that.

With the room so quiet, I hear the lurch and crank of the elevator whirring up through the walls of our building. It's a sound you get used to and forget until you hear it in the middle of the night. Until you realize that your dad might be coming home, which would be a good thing—a great thing—except for the girl. Because I failed to tell him about her, and he'll be pissed that I didn't take her to the precinct or the hospital more than twelve hours ago in case she was hurt or someone was looking for her.

Then again, he told me not to go out.

Then again, I didn't mention there was a girl.

Besides, she doesn't seem to need a hospital. She seems to need company. She seems to need to be here with me.

I pause, bracing for the elevator doors to open, for Dad's footsteps in the hall, for his key to scratch in the lock and for him to turn the knob of our apartment door. But the elevator stops a floor short, then cranks and lurches again, and the sound disappears down into the walls.

I breathe a sigh of relief. I'll call him first thing in the morning and tell him she's here. Or better yet, I'll take her to the precinct early, and he'll never have to know.

"No," she says, making me wrack my brain for what we were

talking about. "Nothing like that. And I know this sounds weird, Kyle, but I have this feeling . . . like I'm not sure I want to remember."

I don't know how to respond, so I nod and turn up the volume on *Cow and Chicken*. The second episode is on already, the one where Chicken eats caffeinated cereal and goes berserk, so I can't help but laugh and try to relax a little.

The girl walks over and sits down. Next to me, on the couch.

"What's this?" She folds her legs up, crisscrossed, so that her knee in my pajama pants is practically touching my thigh. If Dad walked in now, I could see him totally thinking I'm here with some girl from Stuy, taking advantage of being home alone while the rest of the world is a mess. Then again, if I were, he'd also probably be happy about it and give me a pat on the back. He thinks I'm slow in the girl department. But he doesn't know. I don't tell him much, or talk to him the way I talk to Uncle Matt.

Uncle Matt is different. Laid back and funny. He even spotted me a pack of condoms last winter when I told him I was getting kind of serious with some girl. Said he thought I might need them, and was cool enough not to ask if I ever did. Which I didn't, so they're still unopened in the back of my underwear drawer.

The girl peers sideways at me. "You don't want to tell me what this is?" She indicates the TV.

"What? Oh, yeah, sorry. *Cow and Chicken*."

"Who and who?"

"Cow and Chicken." I laugh. "Don't you know it?"

"I'm not sure. Tell me what it's about."

I stare at her knee, filled with an overwhelming desire to kiss her, which I know is totally inappropriate. I don't even know her name. *She* doesn't even know her name.

"Uh, well, Cow and Chicken are sister and brother and, well, they're not exactly brain surgeons. And there's this guy, called Red Guy, and he's always trying to trick them and get them into trouble. And, they may be aliens. That part isn't so clear . . ."

"Ah, that makes total sense," she teases.

"Ha-ha, I know, right? But I swear that's the premise. It's weird, but funny, which is what I like about it, I guess. I like weird dumb stuff," I say.

"I get that," she says, turning back to the TV, and I'm overcome by the smell of vanilla, or coconut, maybe, or both, which must be our shampoo, but smells so much better in her hair. Or maybe I'm losing it completely.

"I need a drink," I say, standing up too fast. *I'm parched. I'm a man in a desert.* "OJ or soda or something, you want some?"

"Sure. I can help." She starts to stand, but I hold out my hand.

"No, don't! Stay here, I mean," I say, bolting from the room.

In the dark kitchen, the red glow of the baby monitor—the one Mom insists on keeping near Uncle Matt's bed even though the doctors have said he's out of the woods—surprises me. I hadn't noticed it earlier. It must've been on in here all day.

I walk over to it and listen to Uncle Matt wheeze. Every few seconds it sounds like his breath gets stuck, but then he goes back to wheezing again.

When I was born, Mom almost named me Matthew after

him, instead of Kyle after my grandfather. I like Matt better, especially since Mom says I take after him. "Tough enough," she says, "but more important, smart and very kind. The best way to be." I don't know about that, though. I wish I were tougher. Even in the condition he's in now, Uncle Matt is way tougher than I'll ever be.

I lean against the counter and wait for my eyes to adjust. I don't want to turn the lights on. I'm not sure why. Uncle Matt makes a noise in his sleep, and the monitor crackles and the red light blinks frantically before steadying again. I switch it off. Nobody is listening, anyway.

I pull open the fridge for light and grab two glasses from the cabinet, fill them with OJ, tuck a bag of Doritos under my arm, and head back to the living room and the girl.

Out the window,
      red lights pulse
           (blood inching through a tube
                in your
                    arm).
I shake the image away, grasp for something happier:
      (Early morning, a latticework table.
           Fruit trees blooming in a courtyard.
      A celebration, yes!
      A blue Tiffany box and
      champagne in flute glasses,
           laughter . . .)
But the red lights haunt me.
      (Winter brings snow . . .

An ambulance flashing its lights,
A hospital room.
The smell of disinfectant,
      filling my nose.)

I wheel away from the window,
     look for Kyle.
He's been gone too long.
I wonder if he wishes I would go.

By the time I get back to the living room, the credits for *Cow and Chicken* are rolling. Thankfully, another episode comes on. Maybe it's a marathon. A marathon would be so, so good.

The girl stands at the window. I set the glasses on the coffee table and sit on the chair across from the couch. If she sits next to me again, she might actually hear my heart pounding.

I tear the bag of Doritos open and hold them out to her.

"Kyle." She says my name the way she did earlier in my sister's room, a statement, not a question, like she needs to be sure.

"Yeah. Everything okay?"

"Yes." She walks over and takes a few chips from the bag. A commercial for Frosted Flakes comes on and my sister's callback flashes through my brain. It was for a cereal commercial, I think.

I try to imagine what it would be like for Kerri's face to pop up now on the screen, eating Wheaties or Corn Flakes or something, as if she belonged to the fake TV family.

"What?" the girl asks. "You're shaking your head."

"Nothing. It's dumb. I was thinking about my sister."

"What about her?"

"Well, you know how I said she's in LA? She wants to act. She went to an acting camp back in July. My mom is chaperoning." I pause, wondering if she remembers where LA is, which makes it hard to have an easy conversation. And I'm not super-suave at talking to girls in the first place. "Anyway, she's been auditioning for commercials there. Not that she couldn't do that here in the city. But there are more opportunities there or something. And it was part of the whole camp thing. After she completed it, they sent her on a guaranteed number of auditions. And my sister got a callback for some cereal one."

"Oh. I was wondering," she says.

She was? It seems confusing how she can have so many regular thoughts, but not know basic things about herself.

"So, I was thinking it would be weird if she got the part, and then I was sitting here and she came on the screen, like, right in the middle of *Cow and Chicken*."

"That would be weird," she says.

"Right? I know."

"Do you miss them?" she asks.

"My mom and sister?" I shrug. "Yeah, I guess so. My mom is cool. My sister's a pain in the ass."

She laughs a little. "And, your dad?" I look away. It always makes me uncomfortable to talk about Dad. I don't know why. Maybe because it reminds me how I disappoint him. "Where did you say he is now?"

"Now, as in, this second? I didn't. He's, uh, downtown, Manhattan . . ." I'm vague because I'm still not sure what I should tell her. What she remembers from the explosions. What might undo her. "He's working late. Overnight shift. He may not be back tomorrow." I pause, then add, "Because of what happened this morning."

She doesn't react, or ask any more though, just goes back to looking out the window. I walk over and stand next to her, and stare out at the haze of muted lights under the shroud of smoke that hangs over Lower Manhattan. I squint through the darkness, through the thickest concentration of smoke, trying to find the empty spot where the Twin Towers used to be.

"Do you miss them?" I ask, maybe because I'm overwhelmed by it all, and I really want to talk about it with her, with someone. "I mean, I know it's dumb to say you miss buildings and all, and I get that they're inanimate objects that don't really mean anything. But I do. I miss them."

She turns to me, the strangest look on her face, like for a split second she's terrified, like she's about to say something but then stops herself.

"What buildings, Kyle?" she asks.

ILLUSION

I dream of the lake,

of the boy,

of the uncle babbling words.

The lake is blue and clear.

Small silver fish jump,

dragonflies dart and skim on

gossamer wings.

Hover, then

disappear.

Somewhere in the distance, music starts up,

light and cheerful:

          a waltz for flute in A major.

A white bird emerges—a heron!

No,

          a swan.

From the shore, the boy calls to it,

      a quavering *oo-ooo* sound

         and it glides toward him, slow and graceful,

then veers sharply into the

tall grasses.

     The boy turns, confused, to the man in the

         wheelchair,

      who shuffles a deck of cards.

I exclaim at the bird and they turn,

      raise champagne glasses

         high in the air.

I wade toward them

   as the white swan slips away.

         Gone.

A whippoorwill calls from the trees,

distracts me, and

   a plane hums overhead,

      its gray shadow, a bird across the sand.

As I reach the shore, a clap of thunder explodes,

        reverberates,

   and the gray bird shudders and

        plummets

     from

       the

    sky.

A noise wakes me. The elevator in the walls.

The front door opening and closing.

I open my eyes, look at my clock: Barely morning.

The door again. No, not the front door. Maybe the bathroom one.

That, or I'm dreaming.

I go with that and roll over and try to fall back to sleep.

The sky shifts,
navy to slate
    to pink at the
        horizon.
Restless,
I walk to the sister's desk.
The shelf above is a clutter of snow globes.
            I noticed them yesterday.
I pick them up, one at a time,
    shake them, and scatter the snow,
    avoiding one in
        the back row.

After a while, I sit up. I listen for Dad, but hear nothing.

My brain staggers back to yesterday, to last night, to *Cow and Chicken*. The girl and I had watched a bunch more episodes before going to bed. When was that? Only an hour or two ago.

Groggy, I get out of bed and make my way down the hall. Kerri's door is closed, so the girl must still be sleeping. I won't bother her this early. I repeat the rest of the drill, stopping at the guest-room door to check on Uncle Matt. He's asleep, too.

Dad's bedroom door is wide open. Bed still made and un-slept-in.

I make my way back in the other direction, to the living room. The sky is dark, tinged at the horizon with oranges and grays, lightening quickly. Police boats continue to pepper the East River. Smoke still pours up from Lower Manhattan, but now blankets a wide stretch of the city up toward Midtown.

I turn on the television and mute the sound, staring at the silent images: rescue workers moving through debris, walking over smoking concrete beams, whole sections of the framework of the towers visible like hulking, mutilated skeletons. And American flags hang everywhere now, are tied to equipment, and wrapped around workers' heads.

Dad must be ready to drop.

I dial his number from the kitchen extension, taking it to my room so I don't wake anyone. I want to hear his voice, even if I have no idea what to say.

He picks up on the second ring. It's quiet wherever he is, his voice not much more than a whisper. "Kyle, everything okay?"

"Hey, Dad, yeah. Fine. I'm . . . Where are you?"

"Catching a brief rest in St. Paul's. They set up cots here, water, snacks. I'm about to head back to the Pile. You're up early. Figured you'd be sleeping in." He sounds different, but I can't put a finger on how.

"I was," I say. "But I didn't sleep well. Did you sleep? When are you coming home?"

"Not really, and I'm not sure. Most of the unit is staying down here. Maybe not today at all. I spoke to your mother, though. She's doing well." *His voice is definitely strange. Wrong.* "Why? Do you need me there?"

"No, not at all. It's . . . I guess I just wanted to talk to you about some things." *About the girl.*

"Matty all right?"

"Yes . . ." I waver, searching for the right words to spill the information quickly. *I wanted to tell you I brought some girl home. She's been here all night. I'm pretty sure she was at the explosion. She has no memory. She may be suicidal, I'm not sure. But she's nice, and she isn't hurt, and I kind of like her being here.*

Yeah, right.

It sounds idiotic and, worse, naïve. Like the exact kind of thing he would get mad at me for. I had no business bringing her here. Or at least keeping her here. I know enough protocol. I should have brought her somewhere official. At least reported her.

But how do you report someone who doesn't have a name?

"Kyle?"

"Yeah, Dad?"

I'll take her to Mount Sinai. Or the precinct on Gold Street. As soon as she gets up. Never have to tell him she was here. I don't need to bother him with this.

"If the rest can wait, I can't talk here . . . there are guys sleeping . . . trying to. We'll talk when I get home. Figure not for a while, though. I really need to be doing things down here for now. It's the goddamned apocalypse, kiddo . . ." The word Marcus used. His voice catches again. "I've never seen anything close to this in my life . . ."

"I know," I say. "No worries. And, Dad? Be safe."

"You, too, kiddo. You, too." He hangs up.

He hasn't called me kiddo since I was twelve.

SNOW GLOBES

"Eiffel Tower, Paris."

    Shake.

            Snow whirls and blankets a girl in a red beret.

    "Disneyland, Anaheim, California."

    Shake.

            Gold glitter spirals down over Mickey and Minnie

            in front of a magical castle.

A moose on a glacier.

            Shake, and

                    snow drifts down.

"Greetings from Anchorage, Alaska."

    A frost-dusted line of Santa-clad dancers.

"Happy Holidays from Radio City Music Hall."

            My breath hitches as I reach for the one

            in the back row.

"Florida, the Sunshine State."

            Shake.

Orange and yellow dots swirl over a citrus grove.

            (A courtyard of fruit trees,

                    your warm fingers touching my

                    cheek . . .)

Shove it back on the shelf

    before

the dots have

            time

to

        settle.

I flip on my computer and stare out the window until the screen warms up. The sky is starting to brighten.

I search Yahoo for the *New York Times* online. The headlines are crazy. TERRORISTS ATTACK NEW YORK AND WASHINGTON...THOUSANDS FEARED DEAD...BUSH SAYS THOSE RESPONSIBLE WILL BE PUNISHED...

I close the window. My dad has been awake in that for nearly twenty-four hours.

I open a new screen and type in mindless things like, *Who holds the world record for hours awake?* That search takes me to some free, new, research website called Wikipedia, which tells me that a dude named Randy Gardner holds the longest record at 264.4 hours awake. I guess I don't need to worry about Dad in that department, then.

Outside, the roar of a military jet jolts me. It's the fourth or fifth time I've heard one since yesterday. I hold my breath, waiting to see if we're being attacked again, but it must be reconnaissance, because after another few seconds, it's gone.

I type a new search—*U2 Slane Castle*—into the search engine and scroll through a few early fan photos that have been uploaded from the European leg of the *Elevation* tour. I'd give anything to have been there.

After a while, Uncle Matt calls out from down the hall. I know he's just dreaming, because it's all loci stuff. Card suits and grocery lists and names of movie stars.

Still, I close out of the U2 stuff and do what I've done a hundred times since Uncle Matt's accident: research recovery rates from spinal cord injuries. Not that I'm a doctor and can help him.

Still, it gives me hope. Mostly, I read statistics and stories.

But there are plenty of anecdotes about people recovering, walking years after no one thought they could.

I try to picture Uncle Matt healthy again, remember him the way he was five months ago, sitting at his kitchen table practicing his memory drills with me. Like with my music, Dad doesn't get Uncle Matt's whole memory thing. He doesn't get why it's important, or that it's really the thing that defines him. That it makes him more than a cop, more than his job, more than what Dad and Uncle Paul are. It makes him special.

All Dad has is his job. He works, he watches sports, he goes to the gym. I'm not criticizing, but I wish he'd understand me better, care more about the things that matter to me, like the music I play. *Used to play.*

Or maybe he's right, and I should try harder to be more like him. And, yeah, like Uncle Matt, too. Because, face it, as smart as Uncle Matt is, he lives up to the Donohue legacy, also. Or he did. I think of Uncle Matt before, lean and mean from biking and running again after the cold winter, keeping up the whole badass persona. Dad's right about this: I could stand to run, lift some weights, maybe. Bulk up a little and make him proud. But I can't bring myself to do the things that might impress him.

Sometimes I envy Marcus's relationship with his parents, how he has it easier with them because they support every little thing he does. But then I remember how it must have been before, and I know nothing can begin to make up for that.

I open another screen and type in *Ugandan civil war*, thinking of my promise to myself last night. I've got nothing else to do. I might as well start now.

Wikipedia has links to four different wars in Uganda. I click on the first, the Uganda–Tanzania War, but that's too early, so I click on the next one, Ugandan Bush War, and I know right away that must be the one.

The Ugandan Bush War (also known as the Luwero War, the Ugandan civil war or the Resistance War) refers to the guerrilla war waged in Uganda between 1981 and 1986 by the National Resistance Army (NRA) against the government of Milton Obote, and later that of Tito Okello.

Obote. Okello. How come we never studied any of this in history class? It seems important, yet I don't remember learning either of these names.

I read, trying to hold on to the information so I understand, but it's confusing stuff about a whole bunch of fighting factions after the removal of Idi Amin. A guy named Museveni, who challenged Obote's election. And names of some group, that I may sort of remember from history class, like the Popular Resistance Army or the Rwandan Patriotic Front.

There's a whole section about guerilla fighters trying to oust the government run by Obote, and then this:

In early 1983, to eliminate rural support for Museveni's guerrillas, the area of the then Luwero District, including present-day Kiboga, Kyankwanzi, Nakaseke, among others, was targeted for a massive population removal affecting almost 750,000 people. The resultant refugee camps were subject to military control and human rights abuses. By July 1985, Amnesty International estimated that the Obote regime had been responsible for killing more than 300,000 civilians.

I stare at that last number, and then the date. 1985. The year Marcus and I were born.

Yesterday, Mayor Giuliani said that over three thousand people were killed in the attack here. I can't begin to wrap my head around that number, so how does Marcus survive knowing his country lost more than a hundred times that number?

I turn off my computer and crawl into bed, close my eyes and try to sleep some more.

I dress in the clean clothes he washed for me:

> khaki cargo pants,
>
> gray top,
>
> black combat boots,

and leave the other stuff folded on his sister's bed.

At the door of the room, I hesitate,

> deciding.

> I walk back to the bed,

> > pull the upside-down lemon shirt on again.

Something to remember him by.

ID

The smell of brewed coffee wafts into my room.

I yank on a clean T-shirt and sweats, hoping Dad hasn't come home unexpectedly while I was sleeping to find the bird girl in Kerri's room.

I should have brought her to the precinct already.

I should have had Uncle Matt up and dressed.

I stand at my bedroom door, trying to hear if Dad's in the kitchen—or if she is—but it's quiet. Too quiet. I don't hear anyone moving around in there.

Maybe he made coffee and crashed, while he was still waiting for it to brew.

Either way, if he'd seen the girl, he'd for sure have woken me by now. Asked questions, and demanded answers.

Unsteady, I start down the hall.

But he's not in the kitchen.

No one is.

The coffee pot is off and empty, and I'm imaging things.

100 . . . 99 . . . 98 . . .

      Blue pots . . .

       pink peonies . . .

Focus on the numbers,

and start over.

Kerri's door is closed. The girl is still sleeping. I continue to Uncle Matt's room, but he's asleep, too, so maybe it's not as late as I thought it was.

I'm discombobulated. I need to wake up fully, and regroup. I need a shower.

When it's hot the way I like it, I step in, let the water run over me, and try to think. I need to take the girl to the hospital, or to the precinct, but which? She doesn't seem sick or hurt, and at the hospital they'll just leave her sitting alone. I picture her stuck waiting in some cold, sterile corridor, strewn with old people dying, or overflow victims from the explosion. Same with the precinct. Until they figure out who she belongs to, she'll be stuck there, waiting alone.

Then again, I heard on the news that the hospitals are empty. That they waited for the injured, but so far there have only been a few.

The people in the towers? Most of them are dead.

I rub shampoo through my hair and rinse. *Hospital or precinct?*

The real truth: I want her to stay.

85 . . . 84 . . .
    . . . *entrechat, quatre relevé, passé* . . .

At the sink, in my towel, I stare at my bleary reflection in the steamed-up mirror.

What was your original face before your mother and father were born?

If buildings fall, but a girl doesn't remember . . . ?

Knock it the fuck off, Kyle.

I know what I'll do: I'll call Marcus. Tell him about the girl. He's good at problem solving. He'll tell me how to handle things.

I brush my teeth, then gather up the dirty clothes from the floor. I'll also do a load of laundry or two, something productive to show for myself when Dad finally gets home.

As I start to put the clothes in the washer, my eye catches on a frayed, white rectangle of paper near the bottom of the machine, stuck to the side of the drum.

The size of a license. It must fit in the plastic sleeve! I must've missed it yesterday when I put the load through again. I washed it twice, then.

I pull the knob to stop the water from filling the machine and reach in to peel it off. But the prior washings have already turned it to glue. I get most of it off, but bits of it, white scraps, stay stuck to the drum in places. The side facing out is mostly blank. On the other side: words and what's left of a photo.

I think it's her school ID.

I try to scrape off the remaining bits, but they disintegrate in my fingers.

I study what's left of the ID.

The top is more preserved than the bottom, enough so that, on further inspection, I can actually make out a decent amount of the faded letters:

F re l LaGu a igh   ol
of Mu c & rt an P   mi g Ar s

Maybe because I've walked past it a bunch of times, I'm pretty sure I recognize the name.

Fiorello H. LaGuardia High School of Music & Art and the Performing Arts.

It's up near Lincoln Center, where Marcus and Bangor and I go to see movies in IMAX 3D all the time. Not that far from Marcus's apartment.

A photo of the girl looks out at me. It's badly washed out, half the face gone, and her dark hair is really long. But still, I'm pretty sure.

Jesus, I washed her ID. Not once, but twice, on the hottest setting.

What an idiot I am.

I stand up and hold the paper up under the light. Beneath the photo in tiny font is part of a faded Roman numeral:

4. M   CC II

No, not a 4. It's an A. Or maybe an H. Yes, an H.

H. M   CC II

It's not a number, it's her name.

76 . . . 75 . . .

    (the curtain lifts on a lake . . .)

Head down.

Focus.

    Block them from coming.

Keep count.

I slip down the hall with the ID, relieved that Kerri's bedroom door is still closed.

I rest it on the edge of the keyboard, and type in *Fiorello H.*

LaGuardia High School, click on the link, and wait patiently for it to load. In my desk drawer, I retrieve the plastic sleeve tied to the toe shoe charm. Of course, it fits right in.

On the high school's home page is a photo of a beige stone building, stairs leading up to the school. I've passed it before.

I look back at the ID.

H. M   CC II.

How many names start with H? *Heather. Hannah. Hillary.* Not too many. I try to think of more, but they're all too cartoony or old-fashioned, like Hildegard or Heidi. Is Hildegard even a real name?

And the other letters. I squint at them some more, but I'm not even really sure.

I click on the *Students* button on the header at the top of the page, my heart ramping up a little, but that only brings me to a *Log in* button and there's no way to do that without a password. It seems like most of the other buttons require that, too.

I try the *Programs* button, which works without one, so I scan down the list of courses. At *Dance Department*, I stop:

The Dance Department utilizes a rigorous conservatory approach. All full-time instructors have danced professionally with major companies, including: American Ballet Theatre, Joffrey Ballet, New York City Ballet, New York City Opera, Royal Ballet, Dance Theatre of Harlem, Boston Ballet, Alvin Ailey American Dance Theater, Martha Graham Dance Company, Erick Hawkins Dance Company, Merce Cunningham Dance Company, Lar Lubovitch Dance Company, and Twyla Tharp Dance.

I scroll back to the top and click on the button that reads *Apply*:

Acceptance to Fiorello H. LaGuardia Arts is based on a competitive audition and review of student records to ensure success in both the demanding studio work and the challenging academic programs. Candidates in the 8th or 9th grade are eligible to audition.

I look through some of the promotional photo galleries, but I can't find anything clear that looks like her.

I close the window, open a search engine, and type *Amnesia*, and scroll around the results again until I find something that seems new:

Dissociative amnesia is defined by a lack of physical damage to the brain, making treatment difficult. During World War II use of barbiturates and other truth serums were popular. Hypnosis is a popular methodology, but can be viewed as merely lowering the threshold of suggestibility. In many cases, patients were found to spontaneously recover from their amnesia so no treatment was required.

See? She doesn't need a hospital. She'll probably get better by herself.

Precinct it is, then, I guess.

I shut down my computer and slip the ID back into my drawer.

73 . . .

     (A cobblestone terrazzo . . .)

   72, 71 . . .

      (You there, in a suit and tie,

         yelling, and checking your watch,

         a briefcase clutched in your hand.)

Kerri's door is still closed, but I'm restless. A few more minutes, and I'll wake her.

I walk to the kitchen for a bowl of cereal and turn on the small TV on the counter.

Updates crawl along the bottom of the screen. Two men, Port Authority police officers, have been pulled alive from the rubble. President Bush is "confident" that the attacks are the work of Osama bin Laden. Rescue workers have remained at the site overnight. Three hundred firefighters are presumed dead. At least twenty police officers are dead.

Mayor Giuliani has declared all New York City schools closed until further notice. Now I really need to call Marcus. And Kristen. And—*Jesus*—Bangor, and Jenny Lynch.

I turn off the TV, pour myself a bowl of Frosted Flakes with milk, and take that to my room. I'm about to call Mom but it's barely 6 A.M. there, and it's still too early to call any of my friends here, so I pick up the Salinger book instead.

Nine Stories.

I flip through pages. The story I'm up to is called "For Esmé—with Love and Squalor."

I read, finishing that and the beginning of a second story, before Uncle Matt calls out from down the hall.

57 . . . 56 . . .

      (. . . voices, shouting, and

                glassrainingdown.)

"Sorry . . . Ky-uh. Need . . . take a . . . piss. And . . . wan . . . see . . . tee . . . vee . . ."

Uncle Matt tries to nod toward his chair.

"Yeah, sorry! No problem." I switch on his television, pull his chair to the bed, and work to maneuver him into it. "I was up earlier and checked on you, but you were still sleeping. So, I did some school work," I say, wanting him to know that I'm trying to be responsible. "And, I'm going to take the girl down to the precinct as soon as she gets up."

"Guh . . . i-dea . . ." he says. He manages to give me a look of disapproval.

"What?" I say. "I swear, I know I need to. I am. Right now. Even though Dad said not to go out."

I wheel him into the master bathroom, trying not to think about how bad the thought of getting rid of her feels.

I set the rails, leaving Uncle Matt on the toilet, and walk down the hall. I have to do the right thing or Dad will kill me.

I knock softly on my sister's door.

49 . . . 48 . . .

Alone is alone

is alone.

I knock again. She doesn't answer.

I crack the door open and whisper, "Hello?"

47 . . . 46 . . . 45 . . .

The bed is made up, my pajama pants folded neatly on the pillow.

My T-shirt is gone.

The wings are gone.

I run down the hall to the bathroom, though it's clear right away she's not in there. The door is wide open, the green toothbrush I gave her last night still resting on the sink.

Why would she leave without telling me?

I sit on the toilet to think, then figure, screw it. If she's gone, she's gone. I can't do anything about it now. It's her problem, right? Not mine.

Fuck.

I lean back against the toilet tank, and stare up at the ceiling. I can't shake the image of the way I first found her:

On the bridge, in those wings. Covered in ash.

Then, leaning out like she was going to fly.

No, like she wanted to fall.

I sit up straight again and look helplessly around the bathroom, wondering if she left me some clue.

My eyes scan the sink again: green toothbrush, wet washcloth, the hand towel I left on the edge. To the left of the sink, the magazine basket! It juts out of place, just a little from where it normally is wedged against the base of the cabinet.

I drag it over. On top is a June issue of the *New York Insider* with a photo of Washington Square Park on the cover. Stone archway, pink trees in massive bloom. A photo inset of those three asshole prep-school boys who they claim raped that exchange student this past summer.

Was that only a few weeks ago? It was such a huge story back then.

I thumb through the rest of the stack. The usual *People* magazines that Kerri insists on having, a stash of clothing catalogues, and the monthly subscription to *New York* magazine.

I shove the basket back with my foot and stand up. Why can't I be an uncaring asshole like those prep-school jerks? Seriously, why do I have to care about some amnesiac bird girl who doesn't even want to be helped?

It's great news that she's gone, right? She's not my problem anymore. And my dad will never have to know.

I'm relieved, in fact. Good riddance.

So why do I feel so lousy?

37 . . . 36 . . . 35 . . .
Almost to the bridge,
    so close.

The glistening water
awaits.

I run down the hall and dress, then get Uncle Matt from the bathroom. As quickly as I can, I move him back to his chair and down the hall to the living room.

"I have to go out for a minute, Uncle Matt."

My mind races. Should I lie and tell him I'm taking her to the precinct? That way, if I can't find her, he'll never know? *Jesus, Kyle. You've already made a mess. Tell him the truth, and find her. Get her, and then figure out what to do.*

"The girl is gone!" I say, rushing. "I don't know where she went, but I have a hunch. I'll be careful, I swear. I've seen other people out there, Uncle Matt. I need to see if I can find her."

"Ky-uh . . . don . . . go . . . far."

I kiss the top of his head. "I won't. I promise. I'll be back in a few minutes."

Stop counting.
   Breathe.
   Here in the shadow of the stairs.
Here, where it seems familiar.
The stone wall,
      cool on my back,
      soothes.
I pull the snow globe from my pocket and hold it up
into a ray of sunlight,
                  shake it and watch
                  the

little red apples

fall.

Shake it again,

make them whirl,

over

taxis,

and tall

silver

buildings.

A frenzy of red

(Blood,

ash,

and

bone)

drifting down.

SQUALOR

I tear down the stairs and out the front door. The toxic smell hits me as soon as I get outside, fainter in some spots, stronger around corners, as I leave the protection of the buildings. Unbearable when it catches the breeze.

Like tires burning, or hair.

Trying not to gag, I hold my sleeve to my nose till I get accustomed to the smell, and head north on Columbia Heights toward the bridge.

The streets are quiet, morose. Only the occasional straggler now and again, though maybe more than I was expecting. As we pass one another, our eyes catch and we exchange these sad, pathetic smiles, as if we've all lost the same friend.

By Cranberry, I'm sweating. I make the right and slow down. I take off my sweatshirt and tie it around my waist, taking shallow breaths as I glance into building entrances along the way.

Hoping I'll spot her sooner.

Hoping I'm wrong.

I leave the snow globe on the ground,
            a farewell,
and start up the stairs
        to the bridge.

I try to keep my mind off anything but reaching her in time, but find myself thinking about the Salinger story, "For Esmé— with Love and Squalor."

A young man gets an invitation to a wedding. He says he wants to go, but he can't. He says he remembers the bride. Flashback: He's a soldier in England, headed off to World War II.

The man stops in a pub and strikes up a conversation with a girl and her little brother. The girl's name is Esmé, and she seems about sixteen. The brother, Charles, is five or so, and quirky and entertaining. Though the girl is way younger than the soldier, she's sophisticated and sure of herself, and it seems as if he likes her or something.

When they part ways, Esmé gives the soldier an old watch her father gave her, and asks if he'll write her letters from the battlefront. She says she hopes they'll be "squalid and moving."

Fast forward to after the war, and the soldier is all messed up. He's in a hospital of sorts, talking to a friend, and we find out that, even though he only met the girl, Esmé, that one brief time, he can't forget her. He can't get her out of his head.

The first step,
    then another.
    Each brings a bit more calm.
I am empty,
    belong nowhere.
    I am ready to let go.
Halfway up,
    the sun breaks through a cloud,
    spills down, warm
        and
    certain.

I turn left on Hicks, the knot in my gut tightening. Now that I'm close, I can't think of anything except the girl.

The sun drifts in and out of the clouds, beats down every few minutes, so that even with my sweatshirt off, I'm sweating.

I make the right onto Middagh Street, and pick up the pace.

(You touch my cheek.
    "Promise you won't be sad, *Papillon*.")

At Cadman Plaza West, I panic and break into a run.

Odette's wings flutter
as she readies to take the stage.

> ("*En pointe*, *Papillon*!
>
> Arms raised, held back,
>
> chest forward, like this.
>
> Fingers light,
>
> thumb curved,
>
> softly touching the third finger,
>
> Kirov style.")

Done correctly, this gives the appearance
her body is
lifting
into
flight.

I run as fast as I can.

In a last dramatic gasp, she steps up,
into the spotlight,
wings
spread
wide.

It's the only true denouement to the story.

IV

FEATHERS

I reach the underpass, race up the stairs two at a time, praying I'll find her there, that she'll be okay and come home with me.

Someone nearby yells something, but my heart pounding in my ears is the only clear sound I can hear.

At the top, I stop, breathless, and stare.

Fuck!

There is no way the girl is up here.

Two soldiers stand in full uniform, both holding Uzis in their hands. Beyond them: a freaking army tank.

They've blocked off the entire bridge.

Of course they have. The city is on lockdown.

A second thought: What if they shoot? What if I'm breaking some law?

I hold up my hands in surrender, my eyes scanning beyond them just in case she somehow slipped through. "My father's Joint Terrorist Task Force," I sputter. It's stupid, but I can't think of what else to say. Clearly, I don't belong here. But there was another guy down there, at the edge of the overpass, and several people milling in Cadman Plaza. From our living room window, I've seen them out on the Promenade since yesterday.

One of the soldiers moves toward me.

"Sorry, I didn't know . . . I wasn't . . ." I stammer, but then it hits me: They're not here to hurt me. They're here to protect me. *Us.* "I'm trying to find a girl . . . I'm going back home now."

I take a step down, backward, to prove it, craning my neck

to see beyond the tank if I can. But I'm pretty sure she couldn't have gotten past them.

This is a good thing. But, then, where is she now?

I turn and continue down, wracking my brain.

Where else would she go? Jesus, she could be anywhere.

I'll try the park and the Promenade, or maybe she went back to the apartment.

Would she know how to get back there if she wanted to?

I circle back, across Cadman Plaza, toward Middagh, my eyes searching everywhere. In my pocket, my cell phone buzzes. I jump, startled, and yank it out.

"Hello?"

It's Mom.

"Kyle, honey, is everything all right? Where are you? I tried you at home."

"Oh, yeah, hey." My voice shakes, and I'm afraid I might cry. I need to stop. I need to slow down. "I went out for a few minutes, close to home," I say, trying to keep my voice casual. "I needed to get some fresh air . . ." *Idiotic. There's no fresh air out here.* I shouldn't have told her I was outside. That I left. She's going to freak out. "I'm just taking a quick walk to the Promenade."

I feel bad. I never lie to my parents, ever. For good reason. My father is a detective. He taught me early on that lies are almost always illogical and transparent, basically the fastest way to get a person in trouble.

"Kyle, I want you to go home now. There are bomb threats everywhere. It's on the news. The whole city is still in danger . . . Do you understand what I'm saying? I don't care what morons are outside today. Dad says the whole military . . ." She starts to cry, which only makes me feel worse. "I want you to go home right now."

My chest squeezes. "Okay, sorry, I will. I am."

I just need to find the girl.

"Promise me, Kyle. And call me as soon as you get there."

On the far side of the bridge, a man grabs my arm,

stops me.

"Are you okay, sweetheart?"

I nod my head, yank myself free

"Getting some air," I say.

He eyes the wings, the snow globe clutched in my hand.

"Are you sure?"

But I just need to think and get out of here.

At Hicks Street, I change my mind and double back to the bridge.

I know she's there! Where else would she go?

When I reach the underpass again, I stop and look around, panting.

No one.

I'm about to turn back, but a guy calls out: "Hey, kid! Are you looking for a girl? Short hair. Big white wings?"

I nod and he points to the other side of the underpass, to the far-side entrance to the bridge.

I stop and sit on the embankment,

eyes closed,

head to knees,
back pressed against the cool stone wall of the bridge.
("Be strong, *Papillon,*
be brave . . .")
When I hear his footsteps,
I don't have to look
to know it's Kyle.

It's so stupid, but when I see her sitting there like that, in those wings, I start to cry.
Embarrassed, I swipe at my eyes with my sleeve.
I'm so fucking mad.
I'm so fucking relieved.
I'm so crazy happy to see her.

He kneels down, puts his hand on my shoulder,
tries to get me to look at him.
But I don't want to see his face,
fold into myself instead,
feeling lost and broken and
awful.
"Hey, talk to me. Are you okay?"
His voice breaks.
"Please come back with me."

"I've caused enough trouble," she says, shaking her head.
"It's no trouble. I want to help you. I want you to come back with me. I don't want . . . I don't want to be alone in this."
Finally, she stands. Keeps her eyes lowered, but follows.

Under the wings, I notice, she has on my T-shirt. In her hand, one of my sister's snow globes.

"Can I see it?" I ask, tapping on the plastic dome.

She hands it over.

It's Kerri's Big Apple one.

The skyline of New York City.

I follow him like I did before.

    Trusting that he'll know what he knows.

        More than me,

        less than me,

            I don't care.

All there is to do is go with him.

    He's the only thing that feels remotely like home.

SIMPLE TRUTHS

We walk along Hicks Street and, without thinking, I veer us onto Orange Street and we head toward the Promenade. I'll walk us home along there. That way, I haven't completely lied to my mom. That way, if she says something to Dad, I've actually been there.

But when we reach the top of the stairs, I'm immediately sorry I've brought her here.

The railing of the Promenade is plastered with missing person posters, blurred Xeroxed faces or stapled photographs that stare out at me. Mothers and fathers, uncles and aunts. Even a few children. Desperate pleas scrawled underneath:

HAVE YOU SEEN ME? PLEASE CALL.

Tabbed rectangles with phone numbers you can tear off flap in the breeze.

But that's not all. Between sections of posters, threaded through the bars, as well as scattered below, are bouquets of flowers wrapped in cellophane or paper. The ground is littered with flowers, teddy bears, and candles. There must be hundreds of candles, their flames burning invisibly in the daylight.

I scan the Xeroxed faces for one that looks like the girl, but don't see any.

I grab her arm and pull us fast along the Promenade toward the Remsen Street exit, trying not to cry again, not to think of all the people who are missing. Not to think of the people they belong to. Like Bangor's uncle and Jenny Lynch's dad.

Was the girl's mom in those buildings yesterday? Her dad?
What if both were inside?

Toward the end, the flyers give way to a single long banner, a white sheet stretched across a whole section of railing, its bold black letters written in paint or thick marker:

We Are Still Standing

I stop and stare at the words, stark against the smoke that streams up from Lower Manhattan. That whole section of city is blanketed in the haze of it all, the putrid smell of burnt things carried here on the wind.

The buildings are gone, thousands of people are gone, but somehow we're still here. Standing. Dad and Mom and Kerri and me. Uncle Matt, and this girl. Those others around us on the Promenade.

We are here, witnessing, while so many others aren't.
It's as if we've weathered a war.

I keep my eyes down,
    glued to the candles that
        flicker in and
            out.
                (A row of votives . . .
                ". . . returns us to dust . . .").

At the bottom of the Remsen Street stairs, she stops and turns to face me.

"I'm sorry. I appreciate everything you've done, Kyle. Really. But I don't want to go back with you."

"Why not?" I ask, fighting tears again.

"You're so nice . . . It's hard to explain. Hard to help you understand. I just know . . . there are things there—here—" She squinches her eyes shut, presses the bridge of her nose.

"Are you hurt? Do you have a headache?"

"No. It's not that. See, the images, they slip in and out. It was different yesterday. Better. Because they were blurrier. Farther away. But today, this morning, they're pressing in on me." I listen, but don't know what to say. "And I don't want to go to a hospital, Kyle. No matter what, okay?" She shudders. "I won't go to a hospital. Ever."

"Why?"

She shakes her head more forcefully. "Please . . ."

"Okay," I say. "You won't. I promise. But please come home

with me. Where else will you go? I promise we won't go any-where but home."

Her eyes dart to mine. She shakes her head again. "You said a hospital or the precinct. Your father will make me go."

"No, he won't," I lie. "I'll talk to him. But if I promise, you have to promise, too. You have to promise not to disappear again. You have to promise to stay until we figure out what to do."

She nods, her eyes filled with tears. I take her arm to start walking. When she resists, I say, "Please. I can't leave my uncle alone."

At that, she relents, but for the rest of the walk she's silent and withdrawn. I know I should say something, but I haven't got a clue what might help.

"Hey, how about this?" I finally say, a lame idea coming to me when we're barely a block from home. "Tell me something simple about you. Something easy you know or might want to remember. Like, I don't know, what's your favorite food? Or, what kind of music do you listen to? Something like that."

She doesn't answer for a minute, so I feel dumb, worried it may be a bad idea. But as we turn onto my street, she leans against my arm and says, "Cherries, how about? Not the canned kind. Fresh ones, with the stem on. The orangey, tart ones, even better. Rainier cherries, I think they're called."

I smile, relieved. "Cherries. Tell me another thing."

"*Mario Kart*, how about?" she says, brightening. "I think I like to play *Mario Kart* with my friends."

"I have *Mario Kart*," I say. "We can play when we get back. Keep going."

"Sometimes I think of dance steps, I told you that, but by

name. And they don't bother me. They make me happy when I think of them."

"Dance steps," I say. "What are they called?"

She looks at me funny, then stops and says, "Okay. Like this." She moves through a few little steps strung together and names them: "*Pas de couru, tendu effacé* front, beat and return. *Passé* to *effacé* back. *Pas de bourée*." And even though I can tell she's doing them half assed, it's still sort of breathtaking to watch her. I wish I could explain exactly why.

When she stops, I say, "Tell me them again, in order. You named a bunch of them ending with pot of something." She wrinkles her nose at me. "Didn't you say 'pot of something' near the end?"

She laughs. "No. Not pot of anything. *Pas de bourrée*. It's this one." She repeats a step, her foot pointing out in front of her, then quickly crossing behind the other like she's barely touching the ground.

"*Pas de bourrée*," I repeat. "Say the others."

"*Pas de couru, tendu effacé* front, beat and return." She gives me a look, almost embarrassed.

"See? It's good! Tell me what else." I start walking again. "Not dance steps, I mean. Other things that you like, that make you happy."

"Watermelon Blow Pops," she says, definitively. "And, for music, um, Alanis Morissette. All the songs on *Jagged Little Pill*."

"Alanis Morissette?"

"Yes, why?"

"No, she's good. I prefer U2, is all, but I'm not judging."

She smiles and walks closer to me, and I don't try to talk or ask her anything more. This little bit is more than enough for right now.

We walk in past the doorman.

"Hey there, Manny," Kyle says.

When the elevator doors close,

he presses eleven, and turns to me.

"Cherries. You like cherries.

Fresh on the stem."

"What about it?" she asks.

"Nothing," I say. "Just that. You like them. It's something I know about you." She smiles, which feels encouraging, so I go on. "Not only the red kind, but the orangey ones that are more tart and sound like reindeer. Rainier, that's it. Rainier cherries," I confirm.

"Oh-kay . . ."

"And *Mario Kart*. Which we can play later, like I said, since it's not like there are a ton of other things to do."

She watches me now, a new look settling on her face, one I haven't seen from her before. Less sad. A little like she thinks I'm crazy. But something else, too, like maybe she's a little intrigued.

"And dance steps. Pa karu, chocolate fondue," I say, sounding them out. "Face front, and a pot of berets, and, yeah, I know those are all totally wrong. In English, I could do it perfectly. It's no fair holding me to French words."

She smiles bigger. "I'll give you those. They're close enough," she says.

The elevator doors open on eleven, and we walk out.

"Why do you remember all that?" she asks, taking my arm and looking up at me when we reach my door.

"Because you told me. And I wanted to." She looks away, but I tip her face back up to mine, then drop my hand quickly, shoving it back in my pocket. But she keeps looking at me. Now is my chance to tell her the thing I've been thinking since I found her today near the bridge, thinking about her all the way home. Even if the thought of saying it is humiliating. I need to, now, fast, before we go in. "And watermelon Blow Pops, and Alanis Morissette, all the songs on *Jagged Little Pill*. And maybe those are minor, unimportant things," I say, trying not to lose my nerve, "but they're about you, so they're important to me, so I want to hold on to them. Because it matters to me that you're here, and that you came back with me." I let out my breath and wait, worrying, pretty sure I just babbled like a fool.

"I'm scared, Kyle," she finally says. "I'm not sure why, but I am. But I feel safe here with you, at least. And I really don't want to go to the hospital."

"I told you, you won't." I keep my hands jammed in my pockets, even though I don't want to. I want to wrap my arms around her and pull her close to protect her.

More than that, I want to kiss her.

But, no, I wouldn't dare.

THE MEMORY OF THINGS

"Wait here."

I close the door and go to Uncle Matt in the living room.

"I . . . hear. You . . . foun . . . her. Tha's good."

"Yeah. But, she doesn't want to go to the hospital, Uncle

Matt. Or the precinct. I can't make her, and I don't want to leave her there alone. I want to give her another day for things to come back to her. Let her stay here, until they do."

Uncle Matt nods. "Can't . . . say . . . I blame . . . you . . ." he says.

While we're waiting for frozen chicken cutlets to heat up for lunch, I get a pen and a notebook from my bedroom.

"So, that thing I did with the cherries, before, on the way home?" I say, "It's a memory trick. Well, Uncle Matt can tell you better, because it's stuff he taught me before his accident. You know how I told you he's a memory expert?" She nods and sits next to Uncle Matt at the table.

"Was . . ." Uncle Matt mumbles.

"Still is," I say, giving him a look. "It's just a matter of more time."

"Ky-uh . . ."

"Kyle yourself," I tell him.

I sit across from the girl and open the notebook to a blank page. "So, anyway, I thought I'd show you how I did that, and how my uncle studies to memorize lists of things." My eyes go to Uncle Matt, then to the girl. "I'm not nearly as good as he is, though. I'm an amateur, and he's amazing. But until he can show you himself, you're stuck with me. If you want me to show you, I mean."

"I'd like that," the girl says, looking at Uncle Matt, not me.

I've noticed that about her, how she looks straight at Uncle Matt when she's talking, how she includes him like there's nothing wrong with him. None of my other friends—the ones who know him better—do that. It's as if they think because he can't talk too well right now, he can't hear them or be a part of things. But the girl is different. It's like she's not at all put off by how he is.

"Okay, give me a second," I say. Off the top of my head, I write a list of ten random words down the page. When I'm done, I say, "It's just for fun, no pressure or anything, I swear."

Now that I've launched into it, the great idea I thought I had back in the elevator sounds definitively uncool. If I look at Uncle Matt, I'm going to know for sure I'm a dork, and I'm going to turn bright red.

"Okay." I push the list over to her. "I want you to read them aloud. One by one. Take your time."

She looks a little uncomfortable, but does:

"Apple
Watch
Umbrella
Tennis racket
Race car
Basketball
Desk
Earring
Stapler
Bird," she says.

"Good. Now, take a few minutes and try to memorize them in that order. I'll tell you when your time is up. Do your best. Don't worry that you won't be able to remember them all."

I watch her eyes move down the list several times, give her a full minute or so, then take the notebook back again. I know what will happen, because it was the same for me the first time. She'll be lucky if she gets more than four.

"Okay. Recite them back to me."

Her eyes dart to mine, and I look away. I have no idea why I'm doing this stupid thing with her, making a fool of myself in front of Uncle Matt.

"Okay," she says. "I'll try. Let's see. Apple. Watch. Umbrella. Race car. Wait, no, not race car yet. Desk. Is that right?" She rolls her eyes at herself and laughs a little. "That's not right. Desk is near the end. Apple, watch, umbrella is right, though, isn't it?" I raise an eyebrow, and she shakes her head. "Never mind. That was pitiful. Bird is the last one. I remember bird came last."

"Don't feel bad." I turn the list back to her. "I swear that's the best I could do when I started, too."

"And now?"

Without pausing, I say the whole list back to her, eyes closed, in order. "You could add about twenty more objects," I say. "Or, if I were Uncle Matt, at least a hundred more."

She turns to him. "Really?"

"Bah then . . . yeah . . ." he says.

"You still can, Uncle Matt. Maybe you can't *lift* the objects yet, but I bet you could remember them." He makes a sound in his throat. I ignore him. "So, do you want me to show you how to do it?" I ask the girl.

"Please."

"Okay, it seems silly at first, but you have to do what I say." She nods. "Ready? We'll start back at apple. And we'll start with your feet. Imagine your left foot. And picture there's an apple under it." I pause, give her a second. "See it?" She nods again.

"Now smash the apple with your left foot. Make applesauce with it. Go to town on that freaking apple."

She smiles, so I keep going. "Okay, left foot, smashed apple. On to your right foot. Imagine you have a watch strapped around your right ankle. Can you feel it wrapped there? Actually hear it tick. Hear the watch on your right foot go *tick tick*." I see her lips move. "Good, next, then," I say.

"At your knees is an umbrella. You squeeze it between your knees because it's raining, so you need to open it and that's how it opens." She gives me a look like I'm weird, and I give her a look back like, *just go with it*. "Imagine it there, okay? It pops open and the rain goes *plink plink plink* on the umbrella. You could say that when it's raining, you kneed an umbrella." She groans, and I add, "I know, but trust me, a joke makes it easier to remember."

"Even a bad one?" She smiles.

"Whatever."

"Fine, I kneed the umbrella. Now what?"

"Tennis racket, at your hips."

"Oh yeah, right. Tennis racket was next."

"Right. I don't know why it's there, but it doesn't matter. They don't have to make sense as long as you can visualize it. So there's a tennis racket growing right out of your hip bone, right here." I press at my own.

"It must be weird, growing a racket from my hip."

"True, but anyway, it's there, so hit the ball with the racket in your mind. Swing your hips to do it. Feel it physically." She twists her torso in the chair, and I smile now.

"Okay, going up. Your, uh, belly button." I picture her stomach, and then my mind goes to her black underwear with the little blue bows, and I feel my cheeks redden. "Okay, so there's a race car there at your navel, a small red Matchbox car or something, driving right out of your belly button like it's a tunnel."

"Here?" she pushes back from the table and touches the flat part of her stomach. I have to look away but nod. *"Beep beep, honk honk, vroooom,"* she says, making me laugh.

"You're hilarious, but smart. The sound effects are actually a technique. Noises help your brain make a better connection. So, the car noises, the rain, the *tick tick,* those are all for a reason, but if you were in school or something, you could do them silently in your head."

She nods, and for a second I wonder what noises might help her to remember who she is. *A particular song? A garage door opening? The sound of a barking dog?*

"Okay, at your chest," I say, returning to our list, "there's a basketball. That one makes sense, at least. Like a chest pass, you know?" I make the two-handed motion. "In your mind, do a chest pass, then throw it hard. Hear it bounce." She nods like she's got it, ready to move on.

"At your neck is a desk. Like a school desk. Wooden, with a cubbyhole for your books and pencils. The elementary school kind, jutting out of your neck."

"I'm probably going to need an operation for that."

"Ha, yeah, you will. Okay, so, we're almost done. On your tongue . . ." She sticks it out, closing her eyes, which sends this weird wave rolling through me. "On your tongue is an earring. A small earring with a white pearl. Hold that on your tongue." She rounds her tongue a little at the center. "It's tiny, so whatever you do, don't swallow it."

She nods, eyes closed, and her tongue waggles a little.

I think about kissing her again.

When she opens her eyes, I know I'm looking at her funny.

"Next," she says. "Kyle? Next?"

"Right. Your nose—" I glance back at the list. "A stapler. There's a stapler stapling your nostrils together. Pinch it with your fingers, like this. Feel the stapler clamp down."

She pinches her nose. "I can't breeze like zis," she says, her voice nasal like she has a cold.

I roll my eyes. "Okay, last, but not least, your head. On top of your head is a bird. A large, perched bird. It's exotic, with a colorful beak like a toucan. When you nod your head, it flaps off using its big black wings."

When I say the word *wings*, she looks away for a second, but when she looks back, she jokes, "Well, I hope it doesn't poop up there," and Uncle Matt, who I thought was sleeping, laughs.

"And that's it. Okay, now for the test. Are you ready? Start at your left foot and tell me the objects in order. Wait till you see how easy it is."

I can tell she doesn't think she's going to be able to do it, but I already know it will work. It always works. I've done it with a lot of people, and I've never seen it fail.

"Trust me. Go ahead."

"Okay," she says, after pausing. "I do. Apple," she starts, concentrating. "Smashed into applesauce." I smile at the added information, which lets me know she's going to be on a roll. "Watch. *Tick tick.* Wrapped around my right ankle. Umbrella. *Plink, plink,* rain." She sticks out her tongue at me, then says, "Oops, not tongue yet, that equals pearl earring, back to my hip. At which there's a tennis racket." She looks up, excited. "Oh my gosh, this really does work, Kyle!"

"Told you. Keep going."

"Race car, out of my belly button. *Beep beep.* Basketball, chest pass. Desk, out of my neck, nose is nostrils, stapler stapling them shut. Earring on my tongue and, I can't believe it, but, head, bird, giant toucan, pooping on the top of my head!"

"I told you," I say.

She stands and curtsies. And smiles.

And, for one split second, as I look up at her, I forget about everything else except for her and me, and this moment. About the two of us doing this silly little unimportant thing together.

I forget about the planes and the buildings and worrying about my dad.

I forget about Uncle Matt's accident, and that he's stuck in a wheelchair.

I forget the girl is a stranger, and I don't even know her name.

I forget about Jenny Lynch's dad and Bangor's uncle. I forget about Marcus and civil wars in countries far away.

I forget that this day isn't normal, that yesterday wasn't normal, that the whole world as we know it has stopped; that there's a weird, hushed pall across the city. Across the nation. And I forget that, at least here in New York, we don't know when—or if—it will ever be normal again.

For one split second, I forget.

But then she sits down and sighs, and like that, I'm slammed with the memory of things. The cold hard truth that she doesn't belong here with me, that this is just temporary, and if I walk down the hall and look out the window, I'll see that endless sea of smoke still pouring from where the Twin Towers used to stand. I'll turn on the news and be reminded again and again and again.

Yesterday wasn't normal. Today isn't normal. And tomorrow isn't going to be normal, either.

There will be no school for who knows how long, and no way for Mom to get home. And Dad will still be down there, in fallen concrete, looking for the bodies of his friends. Not only are the Twin Towers gone, but two other buildings have gone down. Not to mention the Pentagon and the plane crashed into a field.

And Uncle Matt. I want to pretend, but he's still where he was a month ago. *What* he was a month ago: a speech-slurring, invalid wreck.

And the girl? I don't know the first thing about her. Except cherries.

She repeats the list again, bringing me back. This time she recites it clean, the words without the actions or embellishments, then one more time, maybe for her, or maybe for me, and then she smiles, stands up, and curtsies again. And, even though the moment has passed, I smile, and we all just sit there, content enough over some stupid little trick. Or maybe over ten little things we can remember among so many bigger things we can't, or don't want to, because we need to forget.

Wednesday, Late Afternoon into Evening, 9.12.01

TRUTHS AND OMISSIONS

"Hey, Kyle. It's Dad, checking in . . ."

There's the now-usual noise in the background, the banging and drilling, so I know he's on the Pile and not at St. Paul's. I try to figure out what's best to tell him there, now, versus here, whenever he gets home. *If* he ever gets home.

Someone yells for him—*Tom!*—and I lose my train of thought. He continues, "Look, I wanted to check in, Kyle, see how you're faring there with Matty. If all is okay, I really need to go. I've got my guys buried under here . . ."

My chest squeezes. "It is," I say, quickly. "Karina called. She says she can get here tomorrow. And Mom called, too. They're doing okay. No flights yet, but they're trying. She says they're not sure when flights are going to start leaving again . . ."

"Yeah," Dad says. "I think I'd rather not have them in the air yet anyway . . ." I'm surprised to hear him say that. My dad has never been never afraid of stuff like that. Not before now.

"Are we still . . . are they thinking we'll get hit again? Are we—" I stop to collect myself. "Are we going to war, Dad?"

He's quiet for a minute, and when he speaks again, it's in his softer voice, and it's hard to hear him over the sawing and the banging. "No, I don't think so. Not now. I hope not. Listen, we'll sort it all out. For now, I have to go. I'll fill you in when I get home."

"Okay," I say. "I love you."

We hang up.

Another day not telling him about the girl.

I wander to the living room,
         stand off in a corner watching Uncle Matt.
His wheelchair is parked at the window.
         He's mumbling in that slow, broken way of his.
After a while, I walk over and stand next to him.

"I was watching you," I say,

"before, in the kitchen,

and now, here, in this room.

You were doing the memory thing.

The loci trick.

I could see your mouth moving.

I heard you.

Do it again, Uncle Matt.

I know you can."

He tries to turn his head to see me.

I move around to the side of his chair,

kneel down

so he can see my face.

"I heard you do it," I say.

"I bet it's way too easy for you.

Kyle says you're getting so much better."

I wait, but he doesn't answer.

"How . . ." he finally says,

"Can . . . they do this . . . to . . . our . . . ci-ty?"

I stand back up, put my hand on his shoulder.

Dark scribbles move in, but

I fight them off,

shut them away.

"There are things we can fix," I say,

"and things we cannot."

I hold up Kyle's notebook.

"You can fix this.

Let's start with this list.

Go ahead, please.

It will make me feel better if you do."

He head bobs up again, and

  his eyes meet mine.

    "Bet . . . a-bou . . . wha . . . ?"

"I don't know," I say.

    "Maybe everything."

The girl is in the living room with Uncle Matt.

It's amazing how she is with him, how she genuinely seems to listen and to care.

I try to make out what they're saying, but I can't from where I stand.

I take one step closer, but I don't want her to see me. She's holding my notebook in her hands.

A few seconds pass, then Uncle Matt looks up at her. He recites the list, apple to bird, start to finish, without looking.

WIN BEN STEIN'S MONEY

After dinner, the girl and I play *Mario Kart*. When she goes to shower, I sit on the couch in the living room with Uncle Matt. He's got the TV on, the endless supply of bad news going by in the crawl.

After a while, when I can't take it anymore, I say, "Let's watch something else, anything else, okay, Uncle Matt?" and scroll through channels without waiting for his answer.

But I can't find squat. It's like all the other shows that used to be on are gone. Even the other *news* has disappeared, anything not about Tuesday and the Twin Towers. No toxic mold stories. No Lizzie Grubman and the SUV she plowed into the front door of that nightclub in the Hamptons. No Washington

Square Park rape case with those rich Upper East Side douche bag prep-school kids trying to buy their way out of things. No Robert Blake murder, whoever that dude is. A few days ago, those stories were all you could find on TV. *Dateline. 20/20. Headline News.* Now, all of it's gone. Vanished. Just like the buildings.

Like none of that matters anymore.

I flip to Comedy Central midway through a commercial and wait. An episode of *Win Ben Stein's Money* is on. Perfect. Humor *and* trivia. I don't need to wait for Uncle Matt's confirmation. After a minute, he's blurting broken answers before I have time to even concentrate on the questions.

Why isn't Dad here to witness this and see he's wrong about Uncle Matt? That even if Uncle Matt's body doesn't work so great yet, his brain definitely does. His thoughts are getting clearer every day. And that even like this, he's smarter than any of us will ever be. And, more than that, he needs us. He needs to be here. We can't ship him off to some facility because it's taking him longer than we hoped to get better.

I turn and watch him mumbling answers. He looks so much like my dad. Before the accident, the resemblance was uncanny. Before his face got so thin and his jaw got messed up and broken.

A thick lump forms in my throat. As much as I still love him this way, any way, I miss the old Uncle Matt. We used to be really close. Like friends. We'd hang out some weekends if he didn't have a date or neither of us had other plans. I'd take the subway uptown after school to hang out at his apartment, and we'd get pizza and catch a movie, or rent one and order in. Uncle Matt has an awesome Tarantino collection, so we'd watch *Reservoir Dogs*, *Pulp Fiction*, or *Jackie Brown*.

Me, being Ordell Robbie: *Is she dead, yes or no?*

Uncle Matt, doing Louis: *Pretty much.*

That part slayed us every time.

I slide off the couch and sit on the floor in front of him. "We should do some stretches, or Karina is going to be pissed when she sees you tomorrow." I lift his feather-light leg and hold it out, one hand on his heel, the other under his knee to support things. I try to loosen my grip so that he's holding it there on his own. He fights to without much success.

"You . . . know . . . you cah-not . . . keep her . . . here . . . Ky-uh," he says, his eyes shifting to mine. "You have . . . call . . . Mis . . . Per-suhs . . . Soc-ia . . . Servi-ces . . ."

"I know, Uncle Matt. I know. I will. But on the news they've said thousands are missing. She'll sit there, alone. She completely freaked out on me this morning. Said there was no way she could go to a hospital. She's really scared."

"You . . . dah . . . he kih . . . me . . ." he says.

"Yeah, I know."

"On-y good . . . thing . . . Soc-ia Servi . . . of-fice . . . down on . . . Lafy-eh Stree . . . so . . ."

"So it's closed, right?" He's helping me, telling me that Social Services may be impossible to get to. Giving me the story for when Dad finds out.

"Nah . . . tha there . . . aren't oth . . . branch-es . . ." I nod, letting him know that I understand, lift his other leg, and start the exercises on that side.

"I'll call tomorrow. First thing in the morning. I promise." I put his leg down gently, switch and repeat, right after left, until the phone rings, freeing me of the task.

"I'll get it," I say, being a wiseass. I pat Uncle Matt on the shoulder. "Maybe it's Dad. In which case I'll tell him, before I get both of us in trouble."

Or, better yet, maybe it's someone who's looking for her, calling every number in the city and its suburbs trying to reach her, desperate to claim possession of the girl.

I wrap the towel tightly around me.
The shower was hot,
    the mirror completely fogged.
I could wipe it,
       and see,
       but I don't want to.
Just sit in the fog for a while and
    breathe.

The call is Mom, catching me up on things. They're work-ing on getting home, but there's still no word about when flights will resume.

She asks me a hundred questions: Have I seen Dad? Does he look okay? How is Uncle Matt? Has Karina come? And so on.

I answer them all and tell her about Bangor's uncle and Jenny Lynch's dad. All she keeps saying is "Oh my god. Oh my god." When we hang up, I get Uncle Matt washed up for bed. I wipe his face and neck with a washcloth, change him into paja-mas, and move him into his bed. I'll leave the shower to Karina tomorrow.

I think about Karina, how she comes here every day to do this, how tiring it is, how strong she must be to do it by herself.

As I move back toward my room, I stop, hypnotized, outside Kerri's half-open door.

In the sister's closet, a pair of pointe shoes,
    barely
        broken in.
I slip them on and roll up Kyle's pajama pants,
lace the ribbons around my shins.
From the chair, I take the wings,
    slip the straps over my shoulders.
In my head, music plays:
    violins, double basses,
        piccolos, and
           flute.
I start slowly.
    Tombé,
        pas de bourrée,
      glissade,
        grand jeté.
Confined to the space
    I keep the movements small,
    a walk-through to an
      imaginary libretto.
("Come, *Papillon.*"
    Entrechat quatre relevé.
"I'll show you . . ."
    Passé, closed position . . .
      . . . feel your fingers on my back . . .

"Repeat the choreography,

and hold.")

And hold, I whisper.

And hold.

(I tried, but you left anyway.)

The girl is dancing.

And she's amazing.

I watch as she stretches and dips and turns, the wings rising and falling, the feathers billowing, until she finally folds to the floor.

I shouldn't be watching. I should leave her be. Yet, when she's done, I can't move.

It's the most heartbreaking thing I've ever seen.

I return the wings to the chair,

leave the pointe shoes in the closet,

where I found them.

At the shelf, I pick up the snow globe,

the one with the orange trees in the back.

Shake.

Watch the

sherbet-colored dots

rain down.

(Springtime, and you raise your glass.

Summer, then fall.

Leaves the size of saucers drift down,

brown,

red, and

gold,

decompose and turn to dirt.

I shiver, and you put your thin arm around me.

"It will be spring again soon, *Papillon* . . ."

But I can't remember a winter so cold.)

For a change I can't sleep. I get up and switch my computer on, and search for *Missing teen from Fiorello H. LaGuardia High School.*

A bunch of links with names slowly come up and my heart goes crazy in my chest. But as I scroll through them, none seem to have much to do with a teen girl or the school at all, although some seem recent and connected with the Twin Towers.

My eyes scan the list of matches again, names of people who were in the buildings, worked there, were making deliveries. Names of people on the planes that flew into them. Names of workers at the Pentagon. Names of people on the plane that went down in the field in Pennsylvania. Already, so many names. No wonder no one can find her. The city is full of people looking for people.

Still, where are her parents? Were *both* of them inside those buildings?

Jesus, what if they were?

I slide open my drawer, pull out her ID and hold it up close in the light of the screen, squinting, then relax my eyes to try seeing beyond the faded letters. As if I'm looking at one of those stereograms of dots and squiggles where, if you relax your eyes enough, a whole hidden picture emerges.

H. M   CC II, though I'm really not sure about the c's or the i's.

"You need to report her to Missing Persons, Social Services," Uncle Matt keeps saying. But what if no one is out there looking for her?

I stare at the letters again—H. M␣␣CC␣II—but the closest I get to seeing an actual word is macaroni. Not a likely last name for a person.

I open a new screen and search for *traumatic amnesia* yet again, clicking on links, then closing them, until I get to this one from the *Encyclopedia Britannica*:

> Rarely, amnesia appears to cover the patient's entire life, extending even to his own identity and all particulars of his whereabouts and circumstances. Although most dramatic, such cases are extremely rare, and seldom wholly convincing.

I think of the girl earlier, the way she moved when she danced, graceful and precise, repeating moves as if recalling choreography. She knew exactly what she was doing. *What if she really does know everything? What if she's pretending because she doesn't want to go home?*

I scroll down, taking in the heading labeled *Treatments or Therapies*:

> There are no known therapeutic agents confirmed to prevent or reverse amnesia. Most cases of dissociative or hysterical amnesia resolve spontaneously, either suddenly or over time. Psychotherapy has been demonstrated to be supportive in its initial phase. If memories do not return spontaneously, hypnosis or sodium amytal (a drug that

induces a semihypnotic state) may be used to recover them.

I open another screen and type in *sodium amytal*, which the web quickly tells me is truth serum.

Hypnosis or truth serum. Those are my choices.

Unless she already remembers.

Thursday Morning, 9.13.01

UNCLE PAUL

I wake with a start to the phone ringing.

It's bright out. Morning. I sit up. Confused between reality and dream.

Another ring. No one is answering.

What day is it?

Thursday.

How has it already been two days since the Twin Towers fell?

The phone rings again as I fight to clear my brain.

Who else would answer it but me?

It all comes back to me: Dad, still down at the site. The girl, off sleeping in Kerri's room. Uncle Matt, in his room.

He can only get out of there if I get him.

Not normal, but the new normal.

The ringing stops, then starts anew.

I yank on sweats and run to pick up the cordless extension in the kitchen. The coffee pot is empty and clean.

"Hello?" My eyes go to the clock. It's 7:45 A.M. My whole

body clock is off. I've lost track of where days start and where they end.

"Hello?" I repeat.

"Kyle?"

"Yeah." I rub my eyes.

"It's Paulie." *Uncle Paul.* This surprises me, and also makes me mildly sorry I answered. He's always giving me shit and, worse, he's barely come to see Uncle Matt since he's been here.

"Hey, what's up, Uncle Paul?"

"Hey, kid, how you doing?" *The kid thing again.* "Everything there okay?"

"Yeah, I guess so. I mean, I guess it's okay in the scheme of things, you know? Why?"

Uncle Paul laughs, sort of. No, I hear it now for what it is: He's not laughing. He's trying to make himself laugh. It's some weird, guttural, not-Uncle-Paul-at-all noise that comes from his throat like a sigh. Like he's worried about something.

My thoughts start to race.

"Your pop there, kid?"

"Here? No. I don't think so, why? He's still down at the site, no? Maybe at St. Paul's? He hasn't come home at all."

"Are you sure, Kyle?" He sounds agitated, concerned.

"Pretty sure." I shake off sleep, glancing around the kitchen for signs of him. Definitely no coffee. If he'd come in, there would be coffee.

"Kid?"

I get nervous now, too, because if he's not here, and Uncle Paul is still there, asking where he is, well, I don't want to think about that. "Yeah. I definitely don't think he's here. He said the whole unit was staying down there, until you got as many guys . . . well . . . and that, if he needed to, he'd nap at St. Paul's. The chapel, right? The one across the street from the Pile."

"Yes, I know all that, Kyle. I'm down here. And I'm at St. Paul's. But I don't see him here, and I'm pretty sure he's not on the Pile."

"Really?" *Shit.* "Are you sure?"

"I looked around, but there are a ton of guys . . . I'll get someone to radio him. No worries, Kyle. Everything okay across the river?" But I can't think to answer because my brain is racing with panic and fear. I should get Uncle Matt and tell him.

"Look, really, don't worry. I'm sure he's around here somewhere." *I didn't hear him come in. If he came in, I would have heard him, right? And he'd probably be up now, yelling at me.*

"Hang on a sec, Uncle Paul," I manage, a weird knot settling in my throat. I head toward Dad's bedroom.

As soon as I turn the corner, I realize. *His door is closed. He's home! He's in there, sleeping.*

I run the other way down the hall, to the foyer. *Jesus.* How did I miss it? *His work boots are right by the front door.*

Uncle Paul is going to think I'm a moron.

I swallow hard. "Never mind, Uncle Paul. I think he's here. I'm pretty sure. Hang on another second."

I walk down the hall again, turn the knob to his bedroom door, and push it open gently. Dad is under the blankets, dead to the world, his breath slow and rhythmic. I've never seen him sleep this deeply in all my sixteen years.

I shut the door quietly and head back to the kitchen.

"Uh, Uncle Paul?" I whisper.

"Yeah. He there?"

"Yeah," I say, "I'm an idiot. Sorry." But Uncle Paul laughs. "He's sleeping. I didn't hear him come in. I had no idea."

After I've said the part about him sleeping, I wonder if I shouldn't have, if Uncle Paul will give Dad shit for being home, slacking, in the middle of all this. It would be like Uncle Paul to judge even though it's easier for him because he's divorced, and his kids are grown and out of the house, and he's not taking care of Uncle Matt. He has no one to worry about except himself. "I'll wake him," I say. "He's probably already up. Give me a sec."

"No, Kyle, don't!" he barks, then, "Jesus Christ. Thank God."

And now I get it; I hear it. He's not pissed, or judgmental, or annoyed. He was scared and now he's relieved. He thought something had happened to Dad. Even now it must be dangerous at the site, with fires burning, and bomb threats coming in, and steel and concrete collapsing down.

"Kyle, you still there?"

"Yeah . . . Yes, I'm here."

"Okay, as long as he's home, I feel better. Don't wake him. Let him sleep. We've got plenty of guys down here."

"Okay," I say, "I will."

"Have him call me when he gets up."

"Okay," I say again.

"I love you, kid."

Pause. "You, too."

I hang up and stare at the phone. This is Uncle Paul. No nonsense, no slacking, stop-being-such-a-pussy Uncle Paul. Kyle-should-man-up Uncle Paul. Who just said *I love you* to me.

So, now I get it. Now I fully understand.

Tuesday, and those planes, they've broken something. Permanently. And, in the process, they've changed everything.

And everyone.

PANCAKES

The change I sensed with Uncle Paul, I now see evidenced in my dad, by the fact he's in the kitchen making pancakes on a Thursday morning in September in the middle of the apocalypse. Which is what he's doing by the time I get out of my very fast shower, which apparently took longer than I thought since Uncle Matt is also up, still in pajamas, but at the table, sitting in his chair.

I stand frozen in the entrance, unprepared. A deer in proverbial headlights.

What am I going to tell him about the girl?

He must not know yet, or he'd be reaming me. That's for sure.

I stay put in the hall, trying to sort everything, trying to get Uncle Matt's attention. But his head is down, away from me, focused on the newspaper on the table in front of him.

My eyes dart around to make sure, but there's no sign of the girl. And Kerri's door was closed when I came down the hall.

What if she left again?

I shake off the thought. No. She promised me.

Either way, I definitely need to tell Dad now. And explain how I tried to tell him earlier. Explain how I was planning to call Social Services today.

"Hey, Dad!" I'm about to ramble, just spit it all out when he turns, but the minute he does, and I see how awful he looks,

I can't think about anything else except how relieved I am to see him.

His eyes are red and irritated, shadowed by dark circles. Exhaustion lines every inch of his face. One cheek is bandaged with white gauze, maroon bloodstains seeping through. Another spot over his eye glares at me, black-and-blue and, above it, a deep scratch running across his brow. But none of that is what unnerves me. It's something else beneath the surface. How very beaten down he seems. Don't get me wrong, he's covering, or trying to, by whistling, masking it by pouring batter in the pan. But it's something in his eyes, in the way he stands, hunch-shouldered, and worn.

Without thinking, I walk over and he drops the spatula and puts his arms around me. I lean against him, my forehead to his chest, like I used to when I was little. For just a moment, he strokes the back of my hair.

My father, who is not a hugger.

A hiccup shakes his chest.

"Jesus, kid," he whispers into my hair. "You've done good around here."

I nearly lose it when he says that. I squeeze my eyes shut hard, hold my breath, to stop the tears from coming.

When I can, I pull back, and he looks away, too, and nods at the table. "Go on and sit. I thought we all could use some pancakes around here."

I do as he says, sit across from Uncle Matt, where the *New York Times* stares up at him. I spin the paper sideways so we can both see and read the headlines:

STUNNED RESCUERS COMB ATTACK SITES
BUT THOUSANDS ARE PRESUMED DEAD;
F.B.I. TRACKING HIJACKERS' MOVEMENTS.

A photo of rescue workers with masks on, moving around the rubble, fills the folded page. Two other headlines on the page glare up at me: BIN LADEN TIE CITED and A GRIM FORECAST, BAREST COUNT, BY THREE OF HUNDREDS OF FIRMS, HAS 1,500 MISSING.

I turn it back to him and slide the *New York Post* over since Uncle Matt's not reading that one.

Its cover reads SPECIAL EDITION and shows a photograph of three firefighters raising the flag on top of the rubble heap that Dad has been referring to as the Pile. The words . . . *gave proof through the night that our flag was still there* are printed beneath it.

"Shit, Uncle Paul called!" I say, remembering.

Dad doesn't flinch, spatulas another batch of pancakes off the pan, and ladles another batch on, so I tap the table in front of Uncle Matt to get his attention, then mouth, "Is he okay?"

Dad says, "Thanks, I know. I spoke to him. Told him I'd be back down in an hour."

Uncle Matt says, "He . . . jus . . . wan . . . pan-cays. Fig-ure . . . you . . . girl-friend wan . . . some . . . too."

I freak out! I give Uncle Matt my most over-the-top, are-you-fucking-kidding-me look.

Dad turns now. "Oh, that. The girl. Yes, Matty told me about the girl, Kyle." He turns off the stove, carries the plate over, and slides it across the table to me. "Let's talk, okay? Figure things out about her. Before I have to go back to the site again."

A murmur of voices I can't make out from here:

     Kyle. Uncle Matt.

     And, his father.

Kyle sounds different this morning.

     Quieter, less sure.

I stare up at the stars and wait for Kyle or his dad to

                  summon me, and

      tell me it's time

      to go.

Finally, it all spills out in a jumbled foolish rush, exactly how I hadn't wanted it to. I tell Dad everything: how I found her, and how I tried to tell him sooner, but he asked if we could talk later. How after a while, I didn't want to bother him with her since it was clear she was physically okay. That I was going to take her to the hospital, but then she freaked out so much I couldn't bear to, and that I wanted to talk to him about what I should do. That, maybe I was wrong, but I did my best.

Of course, I leave out the wings for now, and maybe the second trip to the bridge, which Uncle Matt knows about, so maybe Dad knows, too. And I leave out the photo ID. No one knows about that.

"A lot of the stuff I've read says her memory will likely come back spontaneously," I tell him. "Most cases resolve in a day or two. I think she's already starting to remember things."

He looks at me hard, then says, "Okay. I get it, Kyle, really. And I feel for her. But you can't ignore procedure. You have until tomorrow then we call MPS, or the department will have my head."

"MPS?"

"Missing Persons," he says. "Meanwhile, when I go back down, I'll at least let someone know at the Pier. They've got a temporary unit down there."

"Okay, thanks."

He raises a brow at me. "Someone could be looking for her, worrying about her, you know."

"She . . ." I say, struggling to find the words. My eyes shift to Uncle Matt because I haven't told him this, either, not exactly. Not what I'm thinking. Or, trying not to think. "When I found her, she was covered in ash. Completely, Dad. Head to toe. I think maybe . . . from things she's said . . . maybe both of her parents were in there. That no one knows she's missing because . . . no one is alive to know." I barely finish the last few words I'm so choked up again. I look away because I can't stop a few tears from slipping out.

Dad reaches across the table and squeezes my shoulder. His arm, even showered and clean, smells strongly of smoke, and from this close, I can see that his nails, the creases in his hands, are still blackened with grit. White bits of ash stick in the line of his lashes.

"Maybe," he says, his voice heavy. "But don't go there yet. Wait it out, and hope for the best, okay?"

"Yeah. I'm trying," I say. I change the subject. "What did you do to your face?"

Dad winces. "Nothing. Got nabbed by a piece of shifting beam." I nod, not letting myself imagine what that means, how unstable it is where he and the others are working. "It's been tough, Kyle, I won't lie. Brutal. Which is why I needed to get home. See you guys, do something normal. Sit and eat a few pancakes with you and my brother, here."

"I hear you," I say, keeping my voice steady for him. "I'm really glad you're home."

He forks a few pancakes from the serving plate onto his own, pours syrup on, and takes a bite, then forks a small piece up and feeds it to Uncle Matt.

"I can do that if you want," I offer. I indicate Uncle Matt's fork.

His eyes shift to mine. "I've got this shift. And, I'll tell you what, kiddo. I'll report her down at the Pier, and I bet someone will come looking for her. And when they do, they'll be very glad to find her alive. Let's go with that scenario. And if no one knows anything down there, we'll call Social Services tomorrow. Now, eat. Go ahead," he says.

I pour syrup and dig in, trying not to look up at him. Because, if I do, there's no way I'm going to keep it together.

Instead, I focus on the pancakes, which are oh-so fluffy and good, moist without being too sweet, like only my dad can make them. After a few more bites, I finally look up again.

"You know my friend Bangor? Alex Barton," I correct myself, realizing Dad might not recognize our nickname for him. "His uncle died in there. And my friend Jenny Lynch's dad, we think, too."

"Christ." He shakes his head and eats another bite before pushing his plate away. "Truth is, Kyle, I have never seen anything like this," he says. "We've lost three in our unit. And Chuck

Simons's son is missing. He responded from the thirteenth. They lost two in their precinct, already." His voice cracks badly now, and he stops. I'm not going to be able to handle it if my dad cries.

Plus, I know Chuck. He's been to our house for Super Bowl games. He's a really nice man.

"His son joined the force last year," Dad continues. "He was a twenty-two-year-old kid." He rakes his fingers through his hair. It's thick and reddish-blond like mine. One of the many physical things we have in common. "They transferred him down to the thirteenth from up in the Bronx two months ago. Two months ago. Imagine! Chuck was so goddamned relieved to have him out of the fucking Bronx. If he had been up there instead . . ." He shakes his head and stands, carries his plate to the sink. "Jesus, Kyle, who would think that Gramercy Park could be more goddamned deadly than the Bronx?"

I don't know how to answer.

He scrapes the uneaten scraps from his plate into the garbage beneath the sink, rinses the syrup, and opens the dishwasher.

"Leave it. I'll do it," I say. He turns and gives me some look I can't read, but I think it's a good one. "All right, I'd better get back down there. Paulie needs to cut out and get some rest, too. So far, I haven't been able to get him to budge. And word is the president is coming tomorrow, so that's good. It'll boost morale." I nod. "That's hush-hush, for the moment, so don't mention it to anyone. We're having a hard enough time protecting the city."

"Okay," I say. "Hey, Dad?"

"Yeah?"

"Karina is coming today. She called to say she'd be here by ten."

"Well, that's something good, right?"

"Yeah. But, well, can I go out at all? Not far. Just for a walk or something. I've been a little cooped up in here."

"To where?" He sounds alarmed.

"Nowhere, I guess. Around the Heights. Even the mayor says we should try to get back to normal."

"Okay, yes," he says. "That's true. But not far. I guess it's safe here in Brooklyn. But not far."

The house smells sweet and delicious, and
        my stomach rumbles.
    I try to think of something else,
     besides hunger and
          leaving.
        Something lighter,
something happy.
I glance at the snow globes, wondering if
       I can still recite the list of things,
       those ten random objects
       from
       memory.
"Apple,"
    I say aloud,
"watch . . ."
and the rest come back to me,
    using Kyle's trick that he learned
from his uncle.
    All the way to bird on my head.

The girl is awake, lying in Kerri's bed.

I wonder what she's heard.

"Do I have to leave?" she asks, worried, when I come in.

"What? No!"

"Oh. I thought . . . I heard you talking to your dad."

"You did," I say. "I was. But he says it's okay if you stay." I don't tell her the rest, about Missing Persons at the Pier, or reporting her to Social Services tomorrow. I don't want to scare her. I'll figure out something new by then if I have to.

"He does?"

"Yes. For now."

"That's really nice," she says.

I laugh a little. "Yeah, well, he's not his usual hard-ass self this week."

"What do you mean?"

"Never mind."

"Oh, and watch this, Kyle!" She sits up, a lightness washing over her, then she starts at *apple* and recites the list I taught her yesterday, fast and easy, finishing at *bird*. "I bet I could do more," she adds, "Fifteen or twenty, maybe." She flashes a huge smile. "It's so cool. I can do it like it's nothing. I don't even have to try."

"See? I told you," I say. "So, anyway, about today, my uncle's therapist is going to be here soon, so my dad said, if we want, we can get out of here for a while."

The lightness shifts to darkness again, a tinge of panic evident in her voice when she asks, "Where to?"

"Nowhere," I say quickly. "I mean, anywhere you want. Within reason. I was thinking maybe a walk on the boardwalk at Coney Island. It's one of my favorite places." And probably way farther than my dad would be okay with us going.

She seems relieved, throws off the blankets and stands. Crossing her arms to her chest, she walks to Kerri's window and peers out. Her short hair spikes out unevenly from sleep in the back.

When she turns and says, "Okay, sure," I can't help it and my eyes go to her chest in my T-shirt, and then, quick, to my sister's desk, where the strap of her bra hangs off the edge of the pushed-in chair. My mind wanders to the little blue bows on her black bikini underwear.

I look away again, force myself to move toward the door. Over my shoulder, I say, "You can shower first if you want. And my dad made pancakes. They're really good. I'll wait for you out there."

"Thanks, that'd be great, Kyle," she says.

Dad leaves for the site, but not without hugging me again.

While the girl showers, I call Marcus, thinking for a minute I'll tell him to meet us in Coney Island. But then I realize that, while the subways may be running in Brooklyn, they're definitely not running in Lower Manhattan. Or from Manhattan into Brooklyn. At least not most of them. Even if they were, I'm pretty sure there's no way Marcus's mom would let him get on one right now.

At the moment, I'm guessing, Brooklyn feels like a whole different continent from Manhattan.

"Hey, mon." He answers on the third ring.

"Did I wake you?" I ask, sarcastically, since it's pretty clear I have.

"No, I'm awake. Going stir-crazy from doing nothing here, you know?"

The girl, standing there braless in my PopMart T-shirt, skirts through my brain. I push her away.

"Yeah, same," I lie. A minute ago I was going to ask him to come with us, so I don't know why I don't just tell him about the girl. "Anyway, checking in. You talk to Jenny or Bangor?"

"I called," he says. "Left a message for her. But I spoke to Bangor. Dude's a mess. I feel for him." I nod, not that he can see me do so. "You call them?"

"No, not yet. Been a lot of work taking care of Uncle Matt," I say, knowing it's an excuse. I haven't called because I'm afraid to. I don't know what to say. "But I'm going to today. This afternoon."

"Sounds good, mon. Call me later, after."

"Yeah, I will. Hey, my dad came home this morning. He's back there now, but he was here. He's doing okay."

"Is good to hear," he says.

"Yeah. But he's a mess, too, Marcus. Banged up and . . ." I realize I won't be able to explain more without getting too worked up. "Anyway, he says he's never seen anything like it. Not in all his years with the department."

"Is so focked up," Marcus says.

"Completely," I say, fighting hard not to let it all come crashing in.

After we hang up, I warm pancakes for the girl. While she's eating, I get another bright idea.

I pull a deck of cards from the junk drawer next to the fridge and say, "Come on, Uncle Matt. This time you're going to show her. Put your money where your big, messed-up mouth is." I give him my best wiseass smile. We always used to joke like that, giving each other shit. I haven't done it much lately. But maybe it's time I do.

At the table, I sort through the deck, self-conscious of how clumsy I am compared to how I know Uncle Matt used to shuffle a deck. I pull out all four suits of face cards, figuring those are the easiest, and we'll start slow. In case he's rusty. I don't want to put pressure on him. Other than yesterday's list of ten, I don't really know what he's capable of.

"Ready?" I say. His eyes slide up to mine, a glimmer of something, amusement or gratitude, I think, held in the look. "Good, then," I say, knowing I might lose it if I look at him again. "Character, action, object, the same way you taught me."

I shuffle the cards again for good measure, and turn the first one over. Queen of hearts. I hold it up in front of him.

"Okay, she's easy," I say, and he says, "Char-ac-er . . . You . . . mah . . ." and I nod because, like always, the queen of hearts is my mom, which is Uncle Matt's doing, not mine. He adores her, and it's mutual. She's always been totally crazy about him.

"Action, flying," I say, trying to focus, "and object, California. So, Mom flying to California, got it?"

"Yes, Ky-uh . . . gah ih. Speed . . . ih . . . up . . . will . . . you?"

"Okay, wiseass. Next."

I flip up the king of diamonds, trying not to let on how happy I feel about Uncle Matt giving shit back to me, playing along.

"Since it's diamonds, we usually try to think of someone rich for any card in this suit," I say, turning to the girl. "Bill

Gates, Warren Buffett, you get the gist. But since it's the king, I'll use Midas. Obvious, I know. The guy who turned everything he touched into gold." The girl nods, forking in another bite of pancake. "So, Uncle Matt, King Midas is the character, the action is easy: counting his money. Actually that's action and object."

Uncle Matt nods. "Speed . . . ih . . . up . . ." he says again.

"And I see you are King Wiseass today," I say, grinning because I can't help it now. Because, for the first time in a long time, it feels like I have a little of the old Uncle Matt back with me.

I flip the next card. "Jack of diamonds. Bill Gates." I lay the card flat. "Action, inventing. Object, duh, a computer. Onward."

I flip again. "Jack of clubs." I turn to the girl again. "Clubs are clovers, so something lucky." *Like you*, I almost say, the thought making my cheeks warm. I keep talking, hoping she won't notice. "We'll make him Uncle Matt's friend Mitch, who once won a ton of money on some game show, right, Uncle Matt? So, character, Mitch. Action, winning. Object, uh, game show, I guess."

The girl reaches out and flips the next card. "Queen of clubs," she says, and smiles, and my heart does a weird little tug. Uncle Matt's eyes shift to mine, and I quickly look away.

"How about you concentrate? Another club. Let's go with Madonna this time. Because she's the literal queen of the dance club. So, Madonna. Dancing. Dance club. Easy, right?"

"Too . . . ea-sy," he says. "Too . . . slow . . ."

"Just like your words, then," I say.

He lets out a laugh. I keep flipping, moving through face

cards and actions and objects. When I've finished all twelve, I hold the stack facedown and say, "Okay, go ahead, big shot. Let's see what you can do."

I hold each card up, facing the girl, so she can confirm as he names them.

"Quee . . . hars . . . fo you ma," he says. "King di-mo . . . jack . . . same . . ." And, before I can turn the next card or the ones after that, he lists them. "King . . . cubs . . . quee . . . cubs . . . Quee . . . spays."

"Well, shit," I say, smiling. "Looks like I'm the dumb one here. You could still do the whole deck, couldn't you, Uncle Matt?"

He nods slowly.

"Am pah-lyze, Ky-uh. Not brain . . . dead . . ."

SVEN

In the bathroom,
> I let my eyes shift to the magazine basket.

I have tried to ignore it since
> yesterday.

Now, I can't. I pick up the magazine on the top of the pile.

New York Insider. June 2001.

I should put it down now.

Kyle is waiting for me.
> But I don't.

I run my finger along the glossy cover, a photograph of a white marble archway crisscrossed by green branches, heavy with pretty pink blossoms.

> A statue of George Washington on either side.

The headline:

THE RETURN OF WILDING MORE
THAN A DECADE LATER.

I let my gaze fall to the photograph
                inset in the bottom corner:
Three boys in white polo shirts
                smiling.

INNOCENT SPOILED RICH KIDS
OR SOMETHING FAR MORE TREACHEROUS?

I press my thumb over the face of the boy,
                the one with the round cheeks and
                                dark brown hair,
                then throw the magazine back as if it burned me.
At the door, I
        turn,
        walk back
        and flip it facedown,
        then go one better and
        bury it
        at the bottom of the basket.

I set Uncle Matt up in the living room in front of the television to wait for Karina, asking too many times if he's sure he'll be okay.

"She'll be here soon," I tell him.

"I'll . . . sur-vi . . . fif-tee . . . min-uhs," he says.

We walk to the subway side by side.
He talks about his uncle, and I listen, but
    the three boys from the cover
        keep drifting in.
    The boy with the cheeks and
        the dark brown hair.
           (Someone shouts and
           a door slams.)
The someone shouting
    is
me.

On the way to the subway, the mist breaks and the sky clears. It's unseasonably warm. The girl takes off her sweatshirt and walks close to me, so close her arm brushes mine. It can almost make me forget everything, to feel her next to me like this. At least until the wind shifts, and the toxic smell bears down, making my eyes burn and my throat itch, and the reality of what's on the other side of the bridge comes slamming in.

If she notices the smell, if it bothers her, she doesn't let on, though her face is knotted in concentration. I want to reach out and take her hand. But I'm supposed to be looking out for her. Not taking advantage.

"What does it feel like?" I finally ask, veering us down the next block. "Like, right now, inside your head? To not know things about yourself?" The second the words are out of my mouth, I regret them. They're stupid. Insensitive. The last thing I want to do is make her feel worse or self-conscious. But I'm sensing some change in her, too, like maybe some details have come back to her, and she's struggling to keep them away.

She crosses her arms to her chest and shrugs.

"I'm sorry. It's—I meant, it must feel kind of weird, right? Like a puzzle missing a piece or something?"

She shrugs again. "It's not that I mind you asking. It's just hard to explain. And I guess I don't exactly want to talk about it now. Is that okay?"

"Yes, of course." I touch her elbow and steer us across the street to the subway station.

We walk down the steps to the train in silence, then she says out of nowhere, "I don't know what I'd have done without you, Kyle. I want to tell you things, give you answers, believe me. I swear I'm not purposely not telling you. You've been so nice . . ." She takes a deep breath and lets it out as a sigh. "So is it okay if we just don't talk about it for right now?"

I nod because it is, but, honestly, the word *nice* eats at me a little. I'm not being nice to her. It's so much more than that.

"Yes, sure," I say, "Anything you want."

The station is shocking when we enter. Not only because it's mostly empty, or because missing persons posters plaster the walls here, too, or because American flags hang in strategic places like penants for the home team, but also because the place is crawling with military. National guardsmen, I think, in camouflage, automatic rifles gripped in their hands.

Two stand at each end of the platform, eyes scanning, and several pace on the opposite side of the platform, as well. It's downright eerie.

The few civilans who are down here with us do that sweet, pathetic smiling thing, like how your mother looks at you if you tell her you've had a fight with your best friend. One woman around my mom's age reaches out and touches my arm, as if to reassure me it will all be okay.

As weird as it is, I feel it, too, the sense that we're all in this together. That those of us who are out and about today are being bold and helpful, because we're going about our lives like Mayor Guiliani told us we have to do.

Pioneers, facing a brave new world.

As we wait for the train, I turn and face the girl. In the yellow lights of the station, tiny droplets of mist sparkle in her short, choppy hair. I think about her photo in that ID, her hair long and pretty, and wonder why she cut it all off. I mean, she still looks pretty this way, but the cut seems hasty and wrong.

"What?" she asks, noticing I'm staring.

"Nothing. I was just thinking."

Out of nowhere there's a shuffling noise, then a loud bang, and I jump, pulling the girl back from the tracks with me. The guards move forward, guns raised, and the woman who gave me the look cries out, but a second later we all see it's only some dude behind us who dropped his skateboard. He picks it up, and gives us a sheepish, apologetic wave, but it takes a whole minute for my heartbeat to go back to normal.

A minute later, lights appear in the dark tunnel and the train comes rolling into the station like always.

The doors open and, for the briefest second, I imagine the girl stepping in, the doors closing, and her riding off without me, never to see her again. I don't know exactly how it makes me feel, or maybe I do, but what I do know is that it seems oddly impossible that two days ago I didn't even know she existed.

How can everything be different now that I do?

Kyle looks at me, but
his thoughts
    are elsewhere.
Maybe he's had enough.
    Maybe he needs me to go.
The look on his face . . .
    there's something pained in it.
I'm making life hard for him.
I should let it all in, tell him everything
    —as if I have that much control.
    Anyway,
      I need one more day of
not remembering.

As we step into the train, I take her hand without thinking. I hope it's okay.

After a second, she squeezes back, and so I'm thinking, *All right, then, maybe it is.*

He takes my hand and holds it tight,
and for the first time in days,
    I feel safe.

There are two other people in our subway car to Stillwell Avenue. This whole freaking city is a ghost town.

One is an older white guy wearing a plain white undershirt, khaki shorts, black socks, and dress shoes. The other is an Indian woman in traditional dress, a floor-length, orange silk thing with black and turquoise threads and mirrored squares, the kind with the fabric that wraps over one shoulder. She has headphones on, and the train is so quiet I can hear sitar music or something like it coming out of them from across the car.

I sit us near the center of the car. We're still holding hands, and I realize I'm squeezing hard, so I loosen my grip, and we sit there, awkward and connected at the same time. The ride is only a half hour but, after a few minutes, my hand gets sweaty, so I figure I'd better let go.

"Did I tell you?" I say, as we leave the dark of the underground terminals and scenery flashes by out the windows. "I read about this guy who had amnesia and—well, first of all, so you know, there are, like, seven different kinds of amnesia. And different degrees of it, too.

"Like, some people can't remember what they did five minutes ago, and each time they do something new, they forget it again. Others might remember everything from when they were little, or from five years ago, and everything from now, but don't remember anything from an entire period in between, as if their mind has blocked out a specific event.

"And still others remember some things from a while ago, but not all things, like, maybe little unimportant things get remembered, while any big, traumatic things are wiped from their memory."

I stop, realizing I've rambled. She looks at me, surprised. "You're quite the expert," she says.

"Yeah, well." I laugh self-consciously, wondering if she's bothered that I've been researching her condition. "Anyway," I say, because I can't turn back now, "there's this story about this guy, and he wakes up from some medical procedure, like a minor operation of some sort, and he suddenly doesn't remember who he is or where he is, or anything. But when the doctor comes to check on him, the guy is speaking Swedish. Only he's not from Sweden, he's American, and his wife says he never knew one word of Swedish before. Not one word. Plus, he says his name is Sven, but it isn't. His name is, like, Bob, or something completely normal like that. Maybe Steven. But definitely not Sven, and nobody knows why he can speak Swedish now, or why his memory disappeared."

She stares at me oddly for a second, then asks, "Did he get it back?"

"I'm not sure. All they talked about in the article was the Swedish-speaking part of the incident."

"That's a great story," she says, and when I try to figure out if she's serious or not, she bursts out laughing. Like doubled-over, hurts-your-stomach laughing. So then I start laughing, so now we both are laughing, until tears are rolling down our faces.

I'm not sure why we're laughing so hard, and I'm not sure she is, either, but it doesn't really matter, because it feels so good to be doing it.

But when I look up, I see the old guy in the undershirt giving us an annoyed look, probably because he thinks we're two punk kids causing trouble, or maybe because he hasn't seen anyone laughing in days.

And then, I realize something else. He could have lost someone. Someone he loves, inside those buildings.

I sit up, sobered, and collect myself, shifting my gaze to him so the girl sees why I stopped laughing. I guess she gets it, because she collects herself, too. She takes my hand again—*she* does—and holds it tight, which is as good as the laughing, or even better. Then neither of us says anything more until the train stops and the guy gets off at the next station.

When the subway doors open at Kings Highway, and the Indian lady gets out, too, the girl leans in toward me, putting her lips way close to my ear. And I'm thinking, *Man, she is going to kiss me,* and I'm waking up pretty much everywhere. But all she does is hover her mouth near my ear for, like, three whole excrutiating seconds before she whispers, "Sven," and we both fall over, cracking up again.

Our moods shift again when we get out on Stillwell Avenue.

The whole area is empty, somber. It's always a little emptier this time of year since the rides on Coney Island close down after Labor Day. But it's a different empty now. Almost nobody is here. The streets themselves are quiet. Those who are out give the same sad, conciliatory smiles or, instead, glance at us suspiciously as we pass by.

And even though the news says that, throughout the country and especially in New York, storeowners should do their best to go about their business as usual wherever possible, the shops here are, for the most part, closed. And, not just closed, but with their metal gates drawn down, triple padlocked with heavy chains. I scan the names of the stores, and then I understand: *Sahadi's Grocery, Damascus Bread, Al Saidi Antiques,* the names repeated underneath in Arabic. And, in their darkened windows, duct-taped cardboard signs, written in Sharpie as thick and bold as possible: *We are FIRST Americans.*

It makes me feel sick to my stomach. Whatever happened Tuesday, we're all *New Yorkers* here.

I push forward with the girl, find her hand again, and squeeze. She doesn't say anything, just links her fingers through mine. As we get closer to the boardwalk, the world feels a little more normal. Nathan's is quiet but open. Any sign of the earlier threat of rain is gone. The sky is a perfect sunny blue. And the smell of burnt things has vanished here, replaced by the smell of french fries.

"You like Nathan's?" I ask, steering us in.

We order hot dogs and fries, douse them in ketchup and mustard, and I pay, then direct us down toward the boardwalk and the water, white paper bag clutched in my hand.

The ocean comes into view,
vast and
    beautiful.
        ("Kick, *Papillon,* kick! Use your arms!
          Close your mouth!
      For Pete's sake, *Papillon,*
        don't drink the water.
          Swim!")

Several people are scattered along the boardwalk, making the world feel a little more normal here. We walk down to the edge of the beach, sit on a bench, and eat as we talk.

"Good?" I ask.

"So good," she says, licking salt off her fingers.

"Have you ever been here?" I nod out over the sparkling Atlantic.

That one she doesn't answer.

When I finish my hot dog, I twist around and look behind us. Off to our right, the bright red Spirograph top of the Parachute Jump juts high above what used to be Steeplechase Park. Behind us, in the other direction, the Crayola-colored Wonder Wheel sits motionless, waiting for next spring.

"I always feel happier here," I tell the girl. "My great-grandpa Jack, my mom's grandfather, he used to have a house in Breezy Point. So he'd take my mom here all the time. Then, when she had us, she took us, too. She's always telling us stories about it."

The girl sits with her legs crisscrossed up on the bench, like she did the first night in my living room. Her knee rests on my thigh. "The Parachute Jump," I say, trying to keep focused, "was defunct even then. It's that one, over there. It was built by the Life Savers Company for the 1939 World's Fair."

"The candy company?"

"Yes," I say, looking at her.

"Okay, go on," she says, taking a big bite of hot dog.

"So it had all these brightly colored rings designed to look like the candies. Anyway, my mom says my great-gandpa Jack and all his friends used to wait in line for hours, like you would at Disney World now. He was in line one night when some couple got stuck on it for five hours, overnight, dangling a hundred and twenty-five feet up in the air. He and lots of other kids stayed camped out in the park to watch the rescue, and he always wished it had been him that got stuck. Because, apparently the stuck couple got sort of famous from it, and one of the perks was that they could always come back for free rides."

"That's it?"

"Yeah, I guess so."

She reaches out and steals one of my fries, though her own bag is full, and says, "Another great story there, Sven."

I'm about to be fake mad, but she leans her head down on my shoulder, and the way she does it, the way it feels, the way she is, I can't explain it, but it makes my heart beat so hard I'm sure she can hear it. It makes me want to hold her and kiss her and know everything there is to know about her. And tell her whatever stupid crap there is to know about me.

"When Kerri and I were little," I say, fighting the urge to wrap my arm around her, "we'd come here with Mom, and she would want to take us on the Cyclone and the Wonder Wheel. Kerri would go on both, even when she was a toddler. But I never would. I was afraid of rollercoasters. Still am, I guess, but now I would go on the Ferris wheel."

"Very brave of you," she says, and I laugh. And then, because I can't not, I touch my lips, just for a second, to the top of her hair. The vanilla scent is strong. I breathe it in, her in, letting it erase everything else, trying to ignore how much I want to do more. And my brain is kind of screaming that I could. I could tilt her face up and kiss her. But another voice is yelling that I shouldn't, because of all the obvious reasons. One, I'm supposed to be looking out for her, not trying to, I don't know, *do* something with her. Two, no matter how normal and good things seem right here, if you pan out with a wide-angle lens, we're in the middle of a disaster. And, three, the truth is, by the time I get to three, I haven't got a clue why I'm counting, why I shouldn't kiss her, and I can barely stop myself from trying.

I stand abruptly, crumpling my hot dog wrapper and half-eaten fries in the bag. "I'm done, you?" I back up toward the trashcan a few feet away.

"Kyle?"

"What? I'm ready," I say, knowing it sounds rude. I feel over-whelmed, like I don't know what's right and what's wrong, like I shouldn't be here, worrying about myself, about how bad I want to kiss some girl, when nothing is right with the world. "You ready?"

"Sure." She follows me over, but I jog back to the bench for my sweatshirt and when I turn around again, she's halfway down the beach, headed toward the water. I chase after her, stop a few feet from where she's kicked off her shoes and tossed of her sweatshirt, and now wades into the surf.

"Hey, Kyle," she calls, "do you swim?"

"What? Yeah. I guess so, but not—" I feel my face change, panicked, as she plunges forward, waist deep, into the waves of the Atlantic.

("Don't be afraid!

Put your face in, Papillon!"

But I'm scared! What if I breathe in the water?

What if I don't come up?

"Oh, but you will. You will, my heart.

I've got you.

You'll be fine as long as

I'm

here.")

The girl wades deeper, disappears completely under as I stand dumbfounded and useless on the shore.

I should go in after her, drag her back, but I don't swim all that well.

The waves swell up, crash back without her onto the shore.

("See, *Papillon*!

Look how brave you are!")

She doesn't come back.

I throw my sweatshirt to the ground and rush into the shallow surf, but I can't see her anymore.

The waves lift me,

fall off again, dropping me

down.

I catch my breath, swim out farther,

past where they break,

and the water is calm.

Here, I float,

let the silence of the water drown out

the sounds

(the tears,

the explosions and

shattering glass,

that still ring

in my ears).

I turn and swim, diving under the water

again and again:

    Let it erase the glazed pots!

    Let it wash away the empty table and chairs!

    Let it scatter the ghosts with

        their bony fingers!

        Let it mask

            their deceitful calls

            from behind velvet curtains,

            and the banks of nonexistent shores.

Let it fill my mouth, and wash away the girl

        who shouts angry words,

            and cruel accusations,

            at a man who can take

        no more.

Let the water overflow,

            and its current

    bring back a distant summer.

    Summer, when the woman's hair

        is lush and long.

    Summer, when pink peonies still bloom on thick green

    stems that

        heave

            with the weight of them.

Let the waves crash down

and obliterate it all.

TETHERED

I stand frozen in the surf, my shirt soaked, my jeans heavy with water.

The wind and salt sting my face.

I'm sure I'll never see her again.

But then, I do. She's swimming back, slowly but surely, toward shore.

I wade out, arms wrapped to my chest,

      clothing weighted and clinging,

      sand pressing through my toes.

Kyle shivers on shore, his face wet with

      seawater, or

      tears.

"Why'd you do that?" he says, when I reach him.

      His voice shakes with fury.

"I'm sorry. I didn't mean to make you mad."

"I'm not mad. You scared me.

      I was fucking scared."

I wipe my nose, push my hair from my forehead.

      He holds his arms out to me.

      I walk forward, and

      let him wrap them around me.

"Don't do it again, okay?" he whispers.

      "I won't. I don't know why I

      had to."

I pull away, look him in the eyes.

      "I'm getting you soaked."

"I'm already soaked," he says.

      Okay, then.

He hugs me back to his chest, and

      I give in and rest my head there.

When we finally get going and reach Nathan's, I usher her inside. "You should use the bathroom in here," I say. "Stand under the hand dryer. Get yourself warmed up, okay?"

"Okay," she says. She starts toward the bathroom, but stops and turns back to me. "I know you must think I'm crazy, Kyle, but before, for those few minutes . . . Well, remember how you asked me earlier how it feels, how I feel, to be me right now? To remember things and not remember?"

"Yes."

"Well, it feels like that, Kyle, back there. Like I'm adrift, in soaking wet clothes that are too heavy with the weight of things I don't even know. And then the water doesn't drown me but carries me and, for a second it lightens everything a little, and I feel momentarily hopeful. But always, there are things, beneath the waves, threatening to pull me under. And the land is right there, close enough to swim to—I can see it—but I'm not sure I want to come back to shore again. It's like I'm here, solid, but I'm not connected to anything. I'm completely untethered. I know that makes no sense," she says.

"It does," I say, "I think I get it. But you're wrong. You're tethered to me."

I order a large Coke and wait for her. When she finally comes out again, she's a whole lot dryer than when she went in.

"You want your sweatshirt back?" she asks, peering up at me.

"No," I say, "Keep it. Come on, swimmer girl. Let's get you home."

LIFE LINES

We head back the way we came, toward the subway.

On Stillwell Avenue, an awning I hadn't noticed on the way here catches my eye. It sticks out because it's purple—a bright pinkish in-your-face kind of purple, like magenta. But it's the neon crystal-ball sign blinking in the window that makes me think about going in.

Not that I think about it too hard. It's an impulse. One I'll probably wish I hadn't acted on.

The sign reads:

Palm Readings.
Tarot Cards.
Hypnosis.
$10.
Madame Yvette.
Come In. Your Future Awaits.

Truth serum or hypnosis.

I grab the girl's hand. "Hey, let's do this," I say. "For the heck of it." But even as I'm saying it, I'm regretting it. Because what if it works and she remembers everything, and then she's ready to go home?

But that's the point, right? For her to remember and go home. For her to be tethered again, to her family. She must have someone, right? So, it's selfish of me to want otherwise.

"I don't know," she says. "I mean, maybe the palm reading thing. I don't like the idea of being hypnotized."

Palm readings aren't one of the cures.

"Yeah, me neither," I say, "So palm readings, then."

And maybe I'm a little relieved.

The door chimes when we open it,
and an old woman ushers us into the back,
    parting a thin burgundy curtain.
It's just a cheap, flimsy thing, but still,
    images slip through my mind.
    I close my eyes to block them,
      block the pieces that
        filter in.

The woman is small and seems ancient. She has a face like an apple carving, pinched and shriveled, sharp features that all but disappear into a series of wrinkles and folds.

She leads us to a small table covered in a cheap, red, velvet cloth flecked with gold. Candles burn on shelves; the smell of incense, too sweet, wafts through the darkened room.

"I'm Madame Yvette," she says. Grasping each of our hands in her bony grip, she turns them over and studies them. She motions me to sit. "You go first. Money up front," she says.

She'd be seriously creepy if I couldn't easily take her with one hand. Maybe no hands.

The girl moves to my side. I try to gauge if she wants to leave.

She gives no clue, so I fish a twenty from my wallet and put it on the table. Madame Yvette sweeps it quickly into a cardboard box.

I look up at her again and she looks away, this time trying not to smile.

Madame Yvette sits and switches on a small green reading lamp. The light is little more than a soft, eerie glow.

"So," she says, "Palm reading, you say, yes? This is your pleasure today?"

I'm not sure about the pleasure part, I think, but she doesn't wait for my answer. Instead she pulls out a deck of cards from somewhere under the table, shuffles them, and places them face-up in front of me. They're not playing cards like Uncle Matt uses, but thick oversize ones with weird and colorful pictures of strange-looking people with sunburst eyes, and trees with snakes wrapped around them. "I like to start with tarot," she says.

"Oh, we were just thinking a palm reading. Right?" The girl rolls her eyes and nods. "Just palms," I say, making it clear.

"Suit yourself." She scoops the deck back, but then stops, lifts the top card, and places it on the table in front of me. "Oh, but we must do this one, because it is very, very good. You should like to know this is your first card."

Madame Yvette taps the card on its drawing of a purple goddesslike woman with flowing hair and gold wings. Behind her, a bright sun rises. Two naked figures stand before her, who look sort of like Adam and Eve. "Ah, see? I knew. I knew." She nods. "I had a feeling about you."

My eyes move to hers, questioningly. "See this? This is why you like to do tarot. Because for you the Lovers come first." Now, I definitely don't look at the girl. My ears must be turning bright red.

"The Lovers are the divine and perfect expression of love, or, in this instance, protection. This is your card. And if I keep reading for you, it will only get better from here." She turns and raises an eyebrow at the girl, as if I'm too thick to get what she's implying.

"That's nice," I say. "But, really, no thanks. I think we're good with only the palm readings."

"It's your money, child. Suit yourself," she says, sweeping the Lovers out of sight.

"Okay. Let's take a look." Madame Yvette holds her hands out on the table, so I place mine faceup in hers. She holds on to my right one and adjusts the lamp with the other, so it shines directly onto my palm. She runs her finger over the various lines.

"This!" she says loudly, startling me, which nearly makes the girl start laughing again. She taps on the most noticeable curve that runs from the base of my palm to between my thumb and index finger. "This is your lifeline. You've heard of that before, yes?" I nod. "Much to the dismay of many a customer, the life-line will not predict how long you will live." I feel relieved at this news, not dismayed.

"The lifeline tells us of other things. Illnesses. Hardships. Tragedy. Heartache. Possibility. It is the story of your life before you walked in this room here, today." Her eyes seek to convey a great gravity, and it occurs to me I shouldn't have brought the girl here. I have an overwhelming desire to get us out.

The woman must sense it. She grips my hand tighter. "Don't be frightened, child. Now, see here . . . ?" She pulls my hand closer and touches a small crisscross in the line at the outside edge of my palm, then shifts her finger the smallest bit. "This is where it starts, and if you follow it to here, at this cross, or *island* as we say, this notch is from when you were a small boy. How old are you now?"

"Sixteen. Almost seventeen."

"Ah, so old? I didn't know. Well, back here, some illness or tragedy befell you, then?" I shake my head, and she says, "I do not mean to you directly, necessarily, but to a treasured loved one, that greatly affected you. Yes, I see it here, I'm sure. Very clearly, at age five."

I swallow hard, wishing she'd picked a different age, any other age that could have left me skeptical and her just some crazy old woman. Six. Seven. Four.

"My Grandpa Kyle died," I whisper. "The night before I started kindergarten."

"See?" she says. "But more than died," she adds, dramatically. "It was a tragedy!"

The crazy old lady is right. We were at his house with my grandmother, having dinner. And he had a stroke right there in front of us. Fell to the floor.

I didn't know what happened. I thought he'd simply fallen asleep, so I thought it was funny, and kept telling my mom to wake him. Until she screamed and started to weep.

I was afraid to go to school after that. Afraid people would simply fall down and die. I missed my first day of school and couldn't sleep for nearly a year.

"He's the one I'm named after" is all I give her.

"Ah, see? No wonder it's so deep, then," she says, tapping the spot on my palm. "There is a very strong connection."

She traces the line forward. "Not so much tragedy since then, though, eh? So it's good." But before I can feel better about her being wrong and a fake, she stops at a spot right past the center of my palm. "Until here. But this is a recent tragedy, yes? A few months ago. In spring. Someone close to you. Not a death, but a terrible, terrible accident."

My eyes go to the girl. She hears it, too, and understands. She shifts uncomfortably.

"My Uncle Matt," I say, my voice shaking. "He got in an accident that paralyzed him."

"Too, too terrible," she says, and makes a *tsk*ing noise with her tongue. "The palms never lie, see? But don't despair. Because, you see here?" She touches a spot a little closer to my thumb. "You notice how it straightens out? This indicates—understand, I cannot make promises, only tell what I see—but here is indication that there will be a great recovery. More than anyone is expecting."

I can't do this anymore. I pull my hand away, my eyes welling.

Madame Yvette waits. "Let me finish. You'll be happy. There is much good news," she says.

I put my hand back and she squeezes it, before tracing the lines again.

"Now, this one." She smiles and traces the curved line that starts near my middle finger and runs to my pinky. "This is a different story. This is your heart line."

Now I really panic. If she can truly see into things, into me, I'm worried what she might say in front of the girl. It was bad enough she said those things about the tarot card.

But instead she says, "People think of the heart line as in romance and ooh-la-la, but, sorry, my friend, it is not." She winks, then, as if reading my mind, adds, "If you want *that* information, I can easily bring back out our Lovers again."

"Maybe another time," I say.

"Whatever you wish. It is your ten dollars. So, the heart line tells us more about one's family, how you were raised, whether you were coddled or not, eh? See the way yours sweeps up in a nice curve? This shows you are loved by your mother and father, am I right?" I nod, but she keeps talking, without needing confirmation.

"But this, this little break here?" She *tsks* again. "This break, the way it wants to lead off your hand here? It shows me you haven't quite found your own love yet." Her eyes go to mine and she must sense me panicking again, because she quickly adds, "For yourself, child. Self love, not outward, is what I need you to understand." I pull my hand back, which she takes as an invitation to grip my chin in that bony hand of hers. She tips my face up. "The line is strong. You have good instincts, but you need to learn to trust in yourself. Not worry about others. Follow your heart."

"Okay, I will," I say, hoping to be done.

"But of course you will!" she says, leaning in to whisper the next part, as if we are coconspirators. "And I suspect this lovely girl here might be the perfect one to help you."

"My hand tells you all that?" I roll my eyes at her now.

"No, sweetheart," she says, a sly smile curling her lip. She nods over at the girl. "Her face does."

The old woman motions for me to sit in Kyle's place.
I don't know that I want a turn,
    that I want to know.
        But I sit anyway.

I hold out my hand.

She traces her finger thoughtfully along each crease, each line,
    then stops, looks up at me, confused.

    "I misunderstood," she says. "You two are related, then?"

I shake my head.

        "Not that we know of," Kyle says.

    "Ah, I see. How strange."

Madame Yvette lowers the lamp, pulls my hand
            closer.

"It's just that this spot here, the island, you see?

    A few months ago, early spring?

    A terrible tragedy. Same exact time as the boy's.

    So I thought, maybe . . ."

I fight not to pull back my hand.

    "But, no, now I see, of course not," Madame Yvette
    continues.

    "This island here

        is much,

            much

            deeper.

    A permanent break in the line."

    Her eyes shift to mine, and she drops my hand.

"Oh, you sweet child.

I'm so, so sorry, my dear."

The girl bolts. I run after her. I finally catch up to her and slow
her down. I don't ask anything. Neither of us speaks much on the
way back down to the subway, or on the ride home. I don't know
what I was thinking, giving Madame Yvette the chance to upset her.

I keep thinking about what the old woman had said, about

how something deeply terrible had happened to her in early spring. Something permanent. Even before Tuesday and the Twin Towers.

Was Tuesday only part of it, then?

Was Tuesday not the worst part?

I try not to think anymore.

POLISH COOKIES

Karina is in the kitchen with Uncle Matt.

"What happen?" she asks, eyeing us with concern. For a second, I'm not sure why she's so alarmed, how she knows, but then I realize how damp and disheveled we both look from our little excursion into the ocean.

"Oh, that. We went to Coney Island," I say. "To the boardwalk." I shoot the girl a look. "*One* of us may have waded in a little far."

The girl gives me a weak smile.

Karina shakes her head like I'm trouble, but we both know she loves me. She's always pinching my cheeks and bringing me stuff she made at home, like special Polish cookies and pies and things. Already I'm eying the plastic tray on the counter, covered in her trademark pink plastic wrap.

She's feeding Uncle Matt lunch, moving his hand to his fork, from there to the plate, like I've been doing, like I've watched her do a hundred times since July. "You do it, Mr. Donohue," she says. "Don't be lazy. Show your nephew how you're the boss. You *make* the hand work for you."

"Maybe he doesn't want to make it work to eat that?" I say, teasing her about the lump of mayonnaise-slathered something-

or-other piled up on his plate. It could be chicken salad, except it has weird yellow chunks poking out of it. "Because if that is pineapple in there . . ."

Karina swats at me, playfully. "Shoo, wise guy! You don't like pineapple? Is a delicious Polish recipe from my grandmother. And you never complain when you eat my *ciastka*."

"*Ciastka*," I say, turning to the girl. "Polish for cookies." I double click the back of my tongue and do that stupid gun thing with my fingers, like I'm something special for knowing a little Polish, and Karina swats at me again.

"You two go get cleaned up. Let Mr. Donohue finish his lunch here. I don't have all afternoon."

Karina's not being hard on Uncle Matt, she's trying to help him. She's good at it, too. "Tough love," she told me the first few days she was here working with him. "He don't need nobody treating him like *niemowlaka*. Baby. He needs to get better, most important."

"He's been talking up a storm," I tell her. "And doing memory tricks," I add, figuring she should know.

She looks up at me. "This is good. Very good. I see this, too. How much clearer he is. Music to my ears, Mr. Donohue." She stands up. "You kids hungry, want to eat?"

I notice Karina accepts the girl's presence without question, and I wonder how much Uncle Matt tried to explain to her. Karina walks over to the Tupperware bowl next to the tray, the one that must hold the pineapple chicken salad, and tips it up to us.

"Uh, no, none for me, thanks," I say. "We ate at Nathan's earlier. If I'd known Uncle Matt was getting *that*, I'd have snuck him a hot dog." Karina waves a spoon at me. "By the way, this is Karina," I say to the girl, "and this—this is my friend."

Some girl I found wearing wings.
Hillary. Haley. Hannah.
Some girl I'm crazy for.

I shake the thought and walk to the tray, peering in through the pink plastic wrap. Karina says, "No touching until you taste the food." She carries the bowl of pineappled chicken back to the table. "Sit, then," she says.

"No, thanks," I say again, but the girl sits next to Uncle Matt and starts asking him questions about his morning.

As he answers her in slow motion, Karina spoons chicken salad onto her plate. When she stops, the girl takes a bite and says, "Oh, man, this is delicious. You should try some, Kyle."

I shake my head and walk to the bathroom to wash up, the whole time thinking how doomed I am.

Seriously, doomed.

Because I'm pretty sure I'm falling in love with her.

ACHTUNG BABY

I take a leak, then, instead of returning to the kitchen, I go to my bedroom and lie down. Suddenly, I'm beyond tired and can't keep my eyes open.

I let them close and let the morning wash over me, Karina's voice drifting in now and again through my half-open door. The girl laughs at whatever she's saying. I think of her laughing at my Sven story on the subway, her hand in mine. Then, down at the shore, disappearing under the waves. The way she buried her head in my chest when she came out, let me wrap my arms around her. And how her wet hair still smelled of vanilla through the salt water. The look on her face when Madame

Yvette said that thing about her deep and terrible tragedy, one that happened around the very same time as Uncle Matt's accident.

"What a shame, eh?" Karina's voice drifts in again, "Terrorists. Who ever hears of such a thing? We never had terrorists in my country, not when I was a girl. Only here, now, in America. In this world. *Zwariowałeś.*" There's a pause, then the girl coughs, and her chair scrapes, and I hear her footsteps move down the hall.

The bathroom door closes and the shower runs.

Karina continues, "*Strugać wariata.* Crazy idiots. The world has gone mad. Come, finish eating, Mr. Donohue. We need you strong and out of this chair."

There's a knock, and I bolt upright.

I've been asleep. I have no idea what time it is.

I glance out the window. Still light, at least. The girl stands at my bedroom door.

Nathan's. Coney Island. Karina.

Has Karina gone home already?

I wipe my mouth with my sleeve and say, "Sorry. I fell asleep. Come in." She steps tentatively in, her hands behind her back.

Is Dad home yet?

How long was I sleeping?

My eyes go to the window again. Definitely still daylight. It's not like me to nap. Everything feels off. I'm so tired. I miss things being normal like they were.

The girl walks over and sits on the edge of my bed, pulls her hands out, and presents two powdered sugar–covered cookies shaped like bow ties.

"*Chrusciki*," she says, struggling to pronounce the word. "Karina said to bring you some. Flour, eggs, sugar, and brandy," she pauses before adding, "*Angel wings*, she called them."

"Brandy," I say, trying not to react to the name of them. "What if I get drunk?"

The girl laughs, and I take one and wolf it down before doing the same with the second. "Oh man, are there more?"

"So good, right?" she says. She's fresh and cleaned up, back in my plaid pajama pants and bare feet—and, now I notice, she has found herself a clean T-shirt. This one is from the *Joshua Tree* tour. "Hope you don't mind. I put a load of laundry in and took this from the clean basket. My stuff was gross, and Karina thought it would be okay."

"Yeah, of course it is." My brain goes to the washer, to the faded ID in my desk drawer, and I imagine bits of white paper winking at her from inside the drum. Then my dumb guy brain skips from that to what's on, or not on, underneath my plaid pajama pants, presuming what little she owns is now inside the washer.

Either way, if she stays here much longer, we're really going to need to get her some new clothes.

"What time is it?" I ask, trying to refocus my thoughts.

"Five."

"Is my dad home?"

"No. But your mom called."

"She did?"

"Yes. But Karina talked to her," she says, hearing my concern. "That was before she went home." I raise my eyebrows, and she adds, "Your mom said to tell you they're working on flights, and that she'll call again later. She thinks they might be able to get out tomorrow."

"Where's Uncle Matt?"

"Karina put him in his room for a rest, said she worked him hard today and tired him out good. Oh, and she said she'll be back tomorrow."

I nod, still feeling fuzzy about it all.

"Hey, are you okay?" she asks. "Am I bothering you? Do you want me to leave so you can rest?"

"No!" I say, too quickly, overeager. "I mean, I'm okay, and no, you're not bothering me. At all. You're the opposite of bothering me."

I look away, embarrased, then get up and move to the window, overwhelmed by it all. Overcome by the constant, growing need I feel to pull her close to me and kiss her.

I need to kiss her really, really bad.

I walk to my desk, grab a box of mints, slip one in, and chew.

"You planning something?" she asks.

"What? No!" My eyes dart to hers, and she smiles, and so now I'm wondering if she's thinking what I'm thinking, if she wants the same thing I do. "I mean, not exactly . . ."

"Kyle . . . ?"

"Yes . . ." I look at her there on my bed, and my brain is yelling things at me, things I can't stop anymore and, more than that, it's reminding me that I may not have too much time left with the girl.

How can I like her so much?

(How can I love her?)

I sit down, leaving sufficient room between us, but reach out and take her hand.

"You snore," she says, finally.

"I do?"

"Yes. A little. Not bad."

She shifts forward, lets go of my hand, and lies back, folding her arms up behind her head. The front of my T-shirt rides up, exposing the soft, flat middle of her stomach. Close enough for me to touch. To lean down and sweep my lips over.

I don't.

I don't want to do the wrong thing.

From where she lies, she nods up at the *Achtung Baby* poster from U2's UK concert, but I can't take my eyes off her skin. "You like them a lot, then, huh?"

"U2? Yeah, I guess I do."

"Who else? What else?" she says. "I'm making a mental list so I can remember." She gives me a smug, playful smile, which fills me.

"Not sure. A lot of artists. Different bands."

"You're truly a great conversationalist," she says.

I laugh, because she's funny, but also because I can't think of words, because all I can think of is what I'm about to do.

And then I do it. I can't help it anymore. I lean down and put my lips over hers. Her mouth parts gently to mine. And, right or wrong, I don't care. We're kissing because I have to.

For a while we just kiss, and everything else falls away, and it occurs to me that, in the middle of one of the worst things that has ever happened to me, is now also one of the best things.

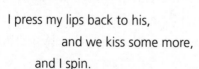

He kisses me softly,
softly,
    softly,
        then harder, but in a
        good way.
Insistent. As if he means it.
    He kisses me like I am here,
        and he is here,
            like he never wants me to go.
And as we kiss, I spin.
I spin and I spin and I spin.
    I'm a jewel-box ballerina,
        and he is the music
        that's winding me.

I stop, move my face away, and say, "I have to tell you something, have to make sure you know."

"Okay," she whispers.

"I get that I don't know you well. I mean, not really, or completely, or maybe at all. But I feel like I do. I feel like I know you more than I should. And I like you. I like you so much more than I'll ever know how to show."

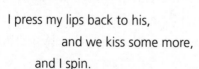

I press my lips back to his,
        and we kiss some more,
    and I spin.

His hands slide around,

slip up under my shirt on my back,

then down around to my sides, to my

bare stomach.

"Can I?"

    He crawls on top of me,

    his body pressed to mine through our clothes.

    And still, I ache

        to be

    closer.

"I think I love you," he whispers, then slips his tongue around

mine.

    The spinning stops, and

    I float,

    a raft, adrift in the water.

    His hands, his words:

the anchor

that holds me here.

I press back, sit up.

Her cheek is damp. She's crying.

I start to ask, but she shakes her head and promises me she's okay.

"They're not sad tears," she says, but I move off her anyway.

I roll to her side, afraid to do too much, or to hurt her, and we lie like that, both of us breathing, her fingers intertwined with mine.

"Are you sure?" I ask again.

"Yes."

She squeezes my hand tighter.

CONVERSATION

The sky outside my window shifts to dusk.

As much as I don't want to, I figure we need to move from here, stop kissing, get up.

I could stay here like this with her forever, but I should probably check on Uncle Matt.

The girl sits up, too.

"So, you never told me," she says, "besides U2, who else do you like?"

I pull out my desk chair and straddle it, facing her. Her brown eyes gaze at me, their amber flecks reminding me of those gemstones you only see sparkle in the right light from a certain angle.

They make me want to go back and kiss her more.

"Okay, let's see," I say, forcing myself to manage a conversation. "I like a lot of different music. Like, I appreciate older stuff, rock, mostly. The Beatles, Santana, The Who. And U2, obviously. Their new album is great, though, so they sort of count as old and new. But I like new-new stuff, too, like Radiohead, or Jamiroquai."

"Who?"

I laugh. "Jamiroquai. They're from London, ethnic funk, sort of. They won a Grammy a few years ago. My friend Marcus turned me on to them." I pop another mint.

"Sing something of theirs for me so I know."

"Not a chance."

"Well, something else, then. A U2 song. Please? Just play it. I bet you're good."

"What do you mean?"

She nods at the corner of my room, behind my desk, where

my untouched Guild sits, gathering dust in its case. It's probably badly out of tune.

"That's a guitar, right? So you must play. So, play something for me. I bet you sing, too." I give her a look now like she really is crazy. "Come on, Kyle, please? I really want you to."

She's not wrong. I used to play in a band. We seriously sucked, and I haven't played much at all since the beginning of last year. I quit after I got tired of Dad and Uncle Paul giving me shit. Even though Uncle Matt said I shouldn't take it so personally.

"My dad wasn't a huge fan of me wasting time on music," I say. "So I haven't played much in the last year. I guess I mess around once in a while on my own, when no one is around to listen . . ." I shut up mid-sentence, because she's walking across my room to the case. She slides it out, removes my Guild, and places it in my lap.

"Here you go. You know you want to," she says.

"I'm not singing, but I'll play . . ." I can't say no to her, no way. Not with the way she's looking at me.

I pull a CD from the stack on my desk and put it in the player. "I'll play you this," I say holding up the case. "It's from their new album."

" 'Mysterious Ways'?" she asks.

I look at her funny, because the song she has named is from, like, ten years ago. "No. It's brand-new. 'Beautiful Day.' From the album *All That You Can't Leave Behind*. Ring a bell?"

She shrugs, so I turn up the volume and wait for the music to start. And then, before I can change my mind, or worry my guitar is out of tune, or care that I'll make a fool of myself because I probably suck for real now, I play. Only a few chords at first, while Bono's plaintive voice sings about skies falling and not letting the beautiful day get away. But without realizing it, after the first verse, I'm singing along, because how can you not when it's U2?

When the song ends, I sit there quiet and a little embarrassed, but she walks over, wraps her arms around me, and says, "Thank you. I'll never forget that, Kyle."

MISSING PERSONS

Dad comes home late looking like crap. Worse than yesterday times ten.

I don't hear him at first, don't realize he's standing there watching me.

I'm in the guest room, getting Uncle Matt ready for the night, struggling to get his pajama pants on, to move him back into his chair. When I finish and turn around, the look on Dad's face nearly makes me break down in tears. It's a look I rarely see. A look that says I'm doing something right for a change.

"Well, I see you've got that down to a science," he says. "I'm really impressed with you, son."

"Thanks, but not exactly," I say, flipping the footrests up, moving Uncle Matt's feet where they belong.

"Don't leh him . . . fool . . . you, Tom," Uncle Matt says. "I dih all . . . the . . . work."

The man who stands in the hallway looks a lot like Kyle.

I watch him through Kerri's half-open door.

They have the same face,

the same red-blond hair,

although his father is
larger.
    But when he turns, I see the difference.
There is something harsh in the father's face.
        Kyle's eyes are kinder and
        more vulnerable.

I introduce Dad to the girl, feeling weird that he hasn't yet met her.

"How are you doing, hon?" He stands at Kerri's door and holds his hand out. "You been cooped up in this purple room?"

She shakes it awkwardly. "No, not at all. Thank you so much for letting me stay here."

He looks her over in my T-shirt and pajama pants and takes in how pretty she is, I'm sure. I'm not sure what else he sees, but I can tell his detective brain is working, the way he's scoping out things. The wings hang on the chair. I wonder if he'll comment on them. Then again, he may not realize they're not Kerri's.

I never did tell him about the wings.

I'm worried he's about to give her the third degree, but all he says is, "Oh, the hospitality part is all Kyle. And, to be honest, probably not the best protocol. But we're all making exceptions this week. We'll have to bring you in sometime soon, though. Someone out there must be very worried about you."

I shoot him a look, anxious for him to be careful what he says, to be vague so he doesn't upset her. "Meanwhile, if there's anything you think of that you want to tell me, please do. Then we can work on getting you back home."

"Okay, thank you." She shifts uncomfortably. "I will."

In the hallway, I ask him, "So, are you home for the night, or do you have to go back down?" He shoots me a look, and I don't blame him. The question comes out way more hopeful than I intended. Of course, I don't want him to have to go back down. But I know better than to try to fix it. I'll only dig myself in deeper.

"I should," he says. "But the president is coming tomorrow, so I have to be cleaned up and back at the crack of dawn. So I'm going to shower and get some shut-eye here. Plus, I have to make a few calls. Reach your mother. Don't know if you heard, but they closed Kennedy and LaGuardia airports again. Sounds like they'll reopen tomorrow, though, and your poor mother is anxious to get home. I'm hoping we can get them on a flight by Saturday. Maybe late tomorrow, if we're lucky. Then again, God knows what security will be like to deal with."

He walks down the hall toward his bedroom, and I follow, my mind racing. Tomorrow is Friday already. I want my mom and sister to come home, and I know the girl can't stay here indefinitely, but I don't want her to leave so soon. I only just met her. Besides, where will she go? How can everything feel so different in a few short days?

"Did you hear anything at the Pier?" I ask, standing at his bedroom door. He strips off his pants and his socks.

"Nothing. No. But it's hard without a name. There wasn't a shred of identification on her? It would sure help a lot if there was."

"Not that I saw," I answer too quickly. He gives me a funny look, but I've waited too long. No way I can tell him about the ID now. Besides, I've looked at what's left of it ten times in the past two days. There's not much to make out, so it's not like the lie is so bad.

Still, I feel guilty, so I'm worried I might give myself away.

He pulls his shirt off over his head and stands there in his underwear. "Man, I stink," he says. "You gonna keep watching me? If so, there's a girl in the house. You may want to close that door."

After he showers, Dad wheels Uncle Matt into the living room and turns on the news.

The black box for Flight 93 has been found.

The White House has declared that the attacks were the work of Osama bin Laden.

All NFL and Major League Baseball games have been called off through the weekend.

And President Bush has announced that tomorrow will be a National Day of Prayer and Rememberance.

I wander down the hall to Kerri's door.

Maybe I can't kiss the girl right now, but I still want her to come be with me for as long as we have left.

Dad puts on *Bowfinger,* an Eddie Murphy movie he loves. He says he's too keyed up to sleep and needs to unwind, watch something mindless for a while. I've seen it before, and I don't think it's nearly as hilarious as he does.

The girl sits with us and watches, next to Uncle Matt, her hand resting on the side of his chair.

I keep looking over at her, wanting to know what she's thinking, if she's thinking about us kissing the way I keep doing, about being together again the way we were.

But she seems oblivious, as if she's content to be watching the movie. As if she's okay with the fact that we're a time bomb ticking, and that in a day or less my mom will be home, and she will likely be gone.

Dad said that tomorrow I have to call Social Services, that we've waited long enough. I wonder if he'll give me until the end of the day.

After a while, I can't take it anymore and excuse myself. Dad gives me a look, but what am I going to say? That I'm in love with some amnesiac bird girl so I can't bear the thought of her going home?

Even I know that's selfish and ridiculous.

I close my door, pick up my guitar, and strum a few scales. I used to practice scales for a half an hour every night, so it all comes back pretty quickly.

I play some more, running through my old set list, wondering if there's any chance I might brush up and audition for this year's jazz band. I have an electric guitar in my closet. Then again, who knows what this school year will look like? Who knows when we're going back to school?

Still, I tell myself, when we do, I might actually try out. I'll have to drag the electric guiter out and mess with it, see how fast it comes back to me.

I take off my jeans and pull on sweats, my eyes going to my bed, to my rumpled comforter. I lie down and get lost in thinking about kissing her.

There's a knock on the door. Probably Dad. I jump up, move my guitar to my closet, grab the Salinger book from my desk, and open it to the middle somewhere.

"Come in," I say. "It's not locked."

Except it's not my dad, it's the girl.

"Mind if I hang out? Your dad and Uncle Matt went to bed. Your dad said he has to go back to work in a few hours."

"Yeah, sure," I say.

What I don't say: *I've never wanted anything so bad.*

I breathe in the smell of his room, of him.

He's the one thing that is solid and certain.

I want to fall into him, on his bed, and let him kiss me again,

but time disappears when I do,

and we don't have much time left.

He thinks I don't know, but I do.

Instead, I walk around his room,

touching his things,

studying them.

Gathering pieces of him to

remember.

She stands at my bulletin board and stares at the photographs there. Walks to my shelves and runs her finger along the spines of the books.

She picks things up and studies them as if she's memorizing information, the feel and weight of them, before putting them back down. I don't mind her touching everything. I like it. It's as if she's leaving her fingerprints everywhere.

But I'd rather she come over here. Let me be with her in the little time we have left.

"Kyle, who's this?"

She lifts a photo in a frame from my windowsill and holds

it out to me. It's from a ninth-grade mixer, me with my arm around Kristen. I'm trying to look all fourteen-year-old big shot and cozy.

"That's my friend Kristen. We dated for, like, a week in the beginning of high school. But now we're just friends."

"Cute," she says, raising her eyebrows.

"Yeah, she still is," I say. "But I swear, we're just friends." As soon as I say it, I feel dumb. She didn't ask me to explain. Besides, I've yet to call Kristen since Tuesday. Or Bangor or Jenny Lynch, for that matter. Jesus, I need to call Jenny. Maybe I'm not such a great friend after all.

"And this?"

She holds up another framed photo, and I laugh. "That's Marcus, who I was telling you about," I say. "He's my best friend."

The photo is from a few Halloweens ago and still one of my favorites, because Marcus and I are dressed so inappropriately. He's a Hershey's Special Dark chocolate bar, and I'm next to him in white, half cut out of the photo, as a Hershey's Cookies 'n' Creme bar. The costumes were his idea. He thought they were a riot. He even brought Hershey's Kisses to hand out to all the girls.

"We thought we were pretty hilarious," I say.

She nods. "I'd like to meet him one day."

"Maybe you can," I say.

Then there's a long silence between us, and I know we're both thinking the same thing. Because what are the chances that she'll even still be here tomorrow, let alone that she'll meet my friends or that we'll hang out together or do other normal things down the road?

Then again, why not? It's not like LaGuardia High School

is in Nebraska. She must live somewhere in New York City. Or, who knows, maybe she lives here in Brooklyn.

She walks over and sits on my bed. I take her hand and squeeze her fingers tightly, then rub my thumb over hers, trying to memorize exactly how it feels.

"I wish you could stay," I say. "I wish things could stay the same."

But I don't really wish that, do I? I want the city to heal, and my mom and sister to come home. I'd miss seeing Marcus. And, I sure want my uncle to get better.

"Don't you want your sister to come home?" she asks.

I laugh for some reason. "Not really. I mean, I'm worried about her and my mom, and I love them, of course, but they'll be home. It's not like they're missing or—"

I stop, horrified. But she doesn't react, simply asks, "But when she's home, you're close with her?"

"With my sister?"

"Yes. Your sister and your mom."

"I guess so. Close enough. My sister is cute, but she's annoying. And my mom, I mean . . ." I don't know what I mean. "I'm a guy," I say, finally. "I mean, she is *nice*. She's a great mom. And usually way nicer than my dad. And she's great at taking care of everyone. Which is why Uncle Matt is living here. She insisted. My dad wanted to move him to a rehab facility, says we're going to have to if he doesn't get better soon . . ." I don't finish the thought. Even starting to say it aloud has caused a lump in my throat.

"You love him a lot, don't you," she asks, "your Uncle Matt?"

"I do, yeah."

"I can see why."

I squeeze her hand harder. And then I don't want to talk anymore.

I shift her down, gently, onto my bed. I lift her shirt, only a few inches, and this time I press my lips to her warm, flat stomach, doing what I've wanted to do since this afternoon.

"Kyle, not too—"

"Yeah, I won't. I swear. Just this one perfect spot, that's all."

I slide my lips back and forth there for a second, then shift myself up so I'm lying on top of her again. I brush my fingers through her short-chopped hair. I stare into her eyes, then press my lips to hers, and kiss her for as long as I can.

Early Friday, 9.14.01

GROUND ZERO

I wake up looking for the girl, remembering she snuck back to Kerri's room sometime after three A.M.

I slink out of my room and hear Dad moving about in the kitchen.

It's barely light out, not even six A.M. I trudge down the hall to the bathroom, feeling groggy and weighed down.

On the way to the kitchen, I slow at my sister's door, fighting the impulse to go in. To crawl under the blankets with the girl, wrap my arms around her, and go back to sleep.

Time is running out. That would only make things harder.

Plus, I should go talk to Dad.

I stop at the entrance to the kitchen, and watch my dad at the table. He's dressed in a suit and tie. It's not often I see him in dress clothes these days. He turns when he hears me.

"You don't need to be up, Kyle. Go back to bed." I nod at his outfit. "President, remember?"

"Oh, right, yeah."

On the table, a special edition of the *New York Post* is open in front of him.

TERROR SUSPECTS ARRESTED.

4 MEN WITH FAKE IDS HELD AT JFK.

"So, they caught them, then?"

"Looks that way," Dad says. "At least some of them."

I pour myself a cup of coffee, and sit down.

"Well that's good news, right?"

He nods. "So, tell me, kid, everything okay with you here? You need anything? Before I head back out again?"

The question takes me by surprise. "Yeah, sure, why?"

"I don't know. I guess I'm a little concerned."

"About what?"

"Well, for starters, it's been a hell of a rough week, Kyle. We haven't really talked about things."

I bring my gaze to meet his, overwhelmed by how hard it is to make eye contact with him.

"Yeah, it has." I want to say more, but I don't know how to put everything into words that make sense. I don't often talk with my dad. "I feel like everything's different," I finally add.

"I hear you on that," he says.

I start to stand, but he puts his hand on my arm. "Give me another minute Kyle, please." I sit again. "So, I'm worried you might have it a little bad for this girl."

Lord help me. I can feel my face grow warm, don't even want to know the shade of red. I should have been more careful, known better than to think I was putting anything past my dad. I slip my arm away, get up, and move to the sink. He lets me go. He could have kept me there easily if he'd wanted.

I'm not sure how to answer, and the truth is, I feel dumb, juvenile, irresponsible, pining away for some girl in the middle of a disaster. He and Uncle Paul are probably laughing about what a lame, pussy loser I am.

"I just don't want you to get too attached, Kyle, that's all. You've got a big heart, and we don't know anything about her. And I've told you, you can't keep her here. I'm going to need to bring her in to Social Services."

"I'm not *keeping* her here," I blurt. "And I'm not attached . . . Jesus, I'm not some lame . . ." But I don't finish, because both of us know that I am.

"I'm not saying that, Kyle. You're a smart, good, awesome kid. But things haven't been exactly normal around here. Which means we need to talk about them. And, suffice it to say, it hasn't gone unnoticed, by me or Matty, that she happens to be a beautiful girl. It would be easy to make it out to be more than it is, to want to hold on to something positive in the middle of all this. Even if you weren't sure what—or who—that something is . . ."

"Give me a break! Jeez!" I slam my mug down. "Sorry, Dad, but please—"

"Fine. Take it easy. I've said what I had to." He gets up, walks over, and cuffs my head and kisses me on the forehead. I want to recoil, lash out at him, tell him to fuck off, but deep down, I know he's hurting, too, and, in his own way, he's trying to help.

"I'm not trying to make you feel bad, Kyle," he says. "I care about you. I'm just looking out for my kid."

I fling myself into the shower.

The water runs over me, hot and cleansing. One of the good things about having Mom and Kerri gone is I can stay in the shower as long as I want to.

As I rub shampoo through my hair, my mind returns to Dad, and the photos in the paper of all those rescue workers standing amid piles of burning rubble, concrete, and steel.

Traipsing over dead bodies, buried in it all.

Ground Zero, they're calling it.

Ground Zero.

I shouldn't have yelled at him. He was worried about me. He was trying to help.

I rinse and lather again, trying to clear my brain of the gruesome images that keep pushing their way back in: twisted bodies, burnt faces, missing limbs.

Is Bangor's uncle in there?

Either of the girl's parents?

Jenny Lynch's dad?

I'm reminded suddenly of the grayscale photos of Nazi concentration camps I came across in a social studies textbook once. Not faded enough to keep me from making out the skeletal bodies heaped in a pile like landfill. Or maybe it was a film we saw in history class, the kind that made one of my classmates woozy—so woozy he'd passed out in the back of the room.

In my head, Ground Zero is like that, heaped with bodies, my father wading through, trying to do his job without breaking.

I adjust the faucet hotter, turning my face to the stream to rinse the soap from my eyes and, of all things, a flash comes to me, of Jenny Lynch's dad.

I met him once! I hadn't remembered until now.

He picked a bunch of us up after a dance freshman year, drove us to a diner in Midtown. He sat in his own booth and drank coffee while the rest of us ate breakfast at midnight. He wouldn't let a single one of us pay. He picked up the whole entire bill.

At the memory, I start to cry.

I cry hard, for a stupidly long time.

When I get out, I call Marcus. It's not even 8 A.M. I'll probably wake him. It's my job, at this point, to wake him.

He picks up after four rings. "Jesus, mon, are you focking kidding?"

"Hey, you sure do sleep well through a disaster."

"I learned young," he says.

I smile, but I know there's painful truth in his joke. Something I understand much better now.

"Anyway, checking in from cheery Brooklyn. Did you ever talk to Jenny? I think I need you to call her first. You're my buffer, man. I realize now I need a buffer. I have no freaking clue what to say to her."

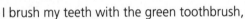

I brush my teeth with the green toothbrush,
> fold his plaid pajama pants and PopMart Tour T-shirt,
> leaving them
> neatly on

his sister's bed.
Pull on my khaki cargo pants,
my gray shirt,
my sweatshirt,
my black boots.
When I knock on Kyle's door
and open it,
he's dressed, too.
"Can we go for a walk?" I ask him.

The girl wants to go back down to the Promenade.

"The place with the candles and the banners," she says.

I ask her to give me a few minutes, and I close my door and call Bangor.

I feel sick when he answers. "Hey, man, it's Kyle. I should have called sooner. I didn't know what to say. I'm so, so sorry about your uncle."

"It sucks, man."

"Understatement." I work not to get choked up. "Let me know if there's anything I can do."

We talk for a few minutes longer then hang up. That was awful, and that was the easy one.

I breathe.

When I'm able, I finally dial Jenny.

While Kyle makes calls,
I sit on the floor of the bathroom and dig through the basket in
the corner.

For the magazine with the boys on the cover.

Before, it made me angry.

Now, it makes me sad.

"I wish I could take it back," I whisper.

Karina isn't here yet, so the girl suggests we leave her a note and bring Uncle Matt to the Promenade with us.

"If he wants to get out for a while, we can manage him, right? We should bring him if he wants to come."

I get him dressed and into his chair, and we maneuver him out of the building, pushing him along the same streets we walked two days ago. But today, in the bleak, gray drizzle, everything looks different, more depressing, so I wonder if we shouldn't have left him at home. Or maybe I'm just being dramatic about everything, knowing that things are coming to an end.

The girl and I don't talk, a safe wedge of distance growing between us.

"Kyle?" she asks, grabbing my arm. "Would you mind if we stop? If I borrow some money? Not a lot. A few dollars. There's something I'd like to get."

I don't know I'm thinking of doing it
        until I ask.
But now that I have, I'm sure.
I feel it in my bones.

It's time.

I guide us away from the Promenade, and take Hicks over to Atlantic.

On the corner, there's an old-fashioned drugstore where my mom shops.

At the door to Heights Apothecary, he stops.

"We'll wait out here. They'll have whatever you need."

He hands me a ten, without me asking.

"Is that enough?"

"Yes, more than enough," I say.

"Thank you, Kyle."

I should say more, because I feel more.

But how will I ever find the right words?

The girl comes out holding a small paper bag.

I don't ask questions, just wait till she's ready and push Uncle Matt with her, toward the Promenade.

As we reach the stairs on Remsen, the rain lets up and the sky starts to clear.

We move Uncle Matt up the ramp and to the railing, the view of Manhattan before him.

Across the river, the plume of gray smoke still billows up from the buildings. Well, from the footprints where the buildings used to be. It seems no less intense than a few days ago.

The ground in front of us remains covered with flowers, with stuffed animals now damp from the drizzle. With wreaths and leis and candles. Of course, most have burned out, so an occasional passerby kneels down to light one, with a lighter he picks up from the ground.

In fact, I notice now that there are lighters everywhere, strewn near the railing for this purpose. A few days ago, those would have been stolen. Taken the minute they were put down. But now they remain. Protected by some unspoken understanding.

We are bound in tragedy, bound against some common enemy together.

Even if we don't know who the enemy is.

As if to confirm this, the number of American flags have multiplied. They hang everywhere, tied to benches and trees, to the railings, flapping wet, yet patriotic, in the breeze. I press the lock on Uncle Matt's wheelchair and put my hand on his shoulder. He shakes his head and says, "Goddamn . . . fuh-kers, Ky-uh." It's the first thing he'd said to me Tuesday morning.

"I know. Come on," I say. "Let's go over to where she is."

Because the girl has wandered away. Not far, and I watched her go. I figured she needed some privacy. But she only moved a few yards down to a section of ground that's less crowded with stuff than where we stand.

I roll Uncle Matt closer, stopping a few feet away.

The girl kneels on the ground. She opens the paper bag, and pulls out two candles, lights them, and says a prayer.

When she's finished, I walk over and hold out my hand.

We leave the candles burning, side by side.

VI

CHANGE

Change comes in two ways. The first is the blindside way that comes without warning. Like Uncle Matt's motorcycle accident. Or the Twin Towers collapsing one Tuesday morning as you're minding your own business in school. Or a girl showing up out of nowhere, covered in ash, and wearing some costume wings.

That kind of change takes your breath away.

But other times, change comes gradually, in that sure, steady way you can sense coming a mile away.

Or maybe a day away.

Or, maybe, a few short hours.

And, since you know it's coming, you're supposed to prepare. Brace yourself against the stinging blow. But just because you plant your feet wider, doesn't mean the blow won't take you down.

I could tell you all the mundane things the girl and I do for the rest of the day trying to prepare, but they don't matter. All that matters is she's still here.

By dinnertime, Dad is home. He chats excitedly with Uncle Matt, over a casserole that Karina made for us, about President Bush's visit. It has boosted morale, he says, given everyone something to work for.

After dinner, he heads to his study to call Mom. Mom, who has a cell phone now. Who, apparently, won't be the last holdout on Earth.

They're at the airport on standby, which doesn't mean much. There's a long waitlist, so they could be there for another twenty-four hours.

The girl has gone to Kerri's room to lie down. I think she needs her space, so I join Uncle Matt in the living room. He's watching some news magazine show, a rerun of *Dateline* from the summer.

I sigh and sit. "This all there is, Uncle Matt?"

Six months ago, he would have tossed the remote at me, said, *Put on whatever you want.*

Now, we both sit and stare.

Onscreen, a reporter stands on a beach doing a story about how the number of shark attacks in the U.S. is on the rise.

"The last thing eight-year old Jessie Arbogast was expecting last weekend as he frolicked on a beach on Santa Rosa Island," she says, "was to be attacked by a seven-foot bull shark while his uncle watched helplessly from shore."

The reporter moves toward the water, hair blowing, mic in hand, and gestures at the wide ocean. The screen turns to white and a title runs: **SUMMER OF THE SHARKS: TREND OR HYPE?**

I vaguely remember hearing about that during the summer, how some kid lost his arm wading in the shallow surf. Soon after, a tourist from New York, vacationing near the Cape, had also gotten bitten while surfing. Beachgoers claimed to have seen a great white shark near the area. It was right before Mom and Kerri left for California, because I remember Dad saying they should both stay out of the water. Then he had hummed the music from *Jaws*, and they had laughed before the two of them launched into some lame old comedy sketch from *Saturday Night Live*.

Dad: (making a doorbell sound)

Mom: Who is it?

Dad: (talking in a weird voice) Flower delivery.

Mom: (looking suspicious) I didn't order any flowers.

Dad: (long pause, funny voice again) Plumber, ma'am.

Mom: I didn't call for a plumber.

Dad: (weird voice) Candygram, ma'am. Candygram.

They both die laughing as Kerri and I roll our eyes.

I ask Uncle Matt if he wants a snack and rummage through the snack closet, deciding on an unopened package of Fudge Stripe cookies. I pour two glasses of milk and stick a straw in one.

"Got milk?" I say, putting his glass on the table in front of him.

I rip open the package and dig in, pulling three cookies out for myself and one for him. I break his into a few smaller pieces, kneel in front of him, and hold out my hand to him. His eyes move to mine.

"Go on," I say. "You know you want to."

"Ky-uh . . ."

I shake my head, but move my hand closer and keep it there, waiting, refusing to do anything to help him.

Tough love.

"I know it's hard, Uncle Matt, but you can."

He opens his mouth to say something, in protest maybe, but then he just lets out a faint grunt, his eyes falling to his own hand in his lap. At first, I think he's annoyed, but after a second I can tell he's actually concentrating.

After another few seconds his hand moves! Only a twitch at first, then a little bit off his lap, into the air.

I hold my breath. Another twitch, and slowly, slowly, shaking from the effort, Uncle Matt brings his hand up and drops it onto mine, slapping the piece of cookie to the floor.

But he moved it! By himself!

"Close enough," I say, trying not to sound too overanxious. I put another piece in my palm, my hand trembling as I hold it out to him. "Go on. Do it again. I know you can."

I see something in him shift, change. He seems determined now, as he makes his hand twitch, then twitch again. Then he raises it slowly, up onto my hand.

I reach out and grab his arm now, to help hold it steady, while he makes his fingers close around a piece of cookie.

"You did it," I say, nodding. "It's good. It's really good, Uncle Matt. I knew you could. It's a start."

I take his hand now and guide the piece of cookie to his mouth. He takes it, lets his head fall back, and chews his reward.

I can't believe it. He moved his hand, his whole arm, on his own! I need to tell Dad!

I say, "I'll be right back, Uncle Matt," my mind buzzing with so much excitement as I stand up to go, that I barely notice what's being said on the television at first. But, then, I do. I turn back and stare at the screen.

It's not the shark story anymore or the female reporter on-screen, but that Stone Phillips guy, the one with the perfect hair. He's talking to a man in a conference room. A lawyer. The shelves behind him are lined with gold-covered books.

The original air date flashes in the upper right-hand corner. *August 18, 2001.*

But it's not the man's voice, or the date, or even his face, that stops me.

It's his name.

What Stone Phillips just called him.

M CC II

I turn up the volume and stand, eyes glued to the set, waiting for Stone Phillips to say his name again.

"Mr. Marconi, as you know, a lot of people are skeptical about this defendant, your client, Mr. Highfront. So, we'd like to hear your side, what led you to take on his matter. Because you have to admit, you're up against a lot of negative public opinion."

Marconi.

Marconi.

I don't hear the name so much as see it, in my mind, broken down into its letters, as if written on a sheet of paper.

A small, waterlogged rectangle, to be more exact.

M CC N I

MARCONI

Marconi.

I was going to tell him, but now it's
too late.

I hear it drift in again from the TV.

My father's voice.

My father's name.

Marconi wears an expensive, dark gray suit and striped tie, has slicked-back black hair and strong features.

Does he look like the girl?

Maybe a little. Who can tell?

But there can't be a hundred Marconis in the world.

The type under him, at the bottom of the screen, confirms it again: David Marconi, Esq., Counsel to Harrison Highfront, III.

"Harrison Highfront," I say to Uncle Matt. "Do you know that name?"

"Wash . . . Square . . . ray case . . . Why?" And now I get what Stone Phillips is talking about. Highfront is one of those prep-school kids accused of raping the exchange student in the park.

The story from the magazine the girl moved.

"Oh, right," I say, trying to sound nonchalant, to keep my voice level until I'm sure.

I walk closer to the television, wondering if Uncle Matt realizes what's going on. But how could he? He doesn't know about the ID, or the photo, or the letters.

I've been withholding all sorts of information.

"If you knew Mr. Highfront like I do," Marconi is saying, "you might not be so quick to judge. But it doesn't matter what you think, or what the public thinks. That's the beauty of our system. A person is innocent until proven guilty.

"My client is entitled to a fair trial based on the facts. My job is to ensure that he gets it. I assure you, Stone, there are facts that we'll present to the jury that you and your viewers don't know.

"For example, I know the press has mentioned my client is an honor student, but did you know he also went to Nicaragua last year with his youth group, to help build affordable homes for the poor? People see his clothing, his house, his background, and they make assumptions. But that's what our legal system is for. To dispel them. Don't let the Polo shirt fool you."

Stone holds up a hand as if he needs to interject, but Marconi says, "No, first let me finish, please. You imply I can't represent this defendant in good conscience, and you wouldn't be alone in your hasty assumptions. But you will all soon see that Mr. Highfront isn't at all who the media has made him out to be.

"He's a good kid, honest and remorseful. He doesn't for a minute deny he was there in the park that night. He doesn't deny that he picked the wrong group of friends, or that he made a deadly decision to stay out with those friends so late.

"But he was not the perpetrator here, I assure you. On the contrary, he was actually a second victim. He fled the scene only after he tried to stop the event from taking place—the evidence will, in fact, show this and more, when we have our day in court.

"I will demonstrate that Mr. Highfront is nothing more than a young man bullied by his peers. Peers who labeled him a coward and hoped to frame him."

Stone uncrosses his legs, leans forward. "With all due respect, Mr. Marconi, isn't that what all defense lawyers say about their clients?"

Marconi doesn't squirm. There's something likable about him, actually. Something I might not have noticed if I had watched this before. He seems passionate and sincere. As if he genuinely believes what he is saying.

"On the contrary, Stone. I've had many clients I have represented to the best of my ability, but, if pressed, I couldn't have said one nice word about them. That is not the case with this young man, I promise you. No one wants the truth to come out more than we do. And one more thing: To the extent Mr. Highfront was present for a single moment of the heinous proceedings, he's deeply remorseful. He wants to right any omission and suffer the consequences. But I'm confident the evidence will speak for itself, that a jury will acquit him when given the opportunity to hear his story in his own words."

There's a long silence during which Marconi seems almost to be moved to tears. When he speaks again, his voice is little more than a choked-up whisper.

"Life is short, Stone, sometimes brutally short, and way too often brutally unfair. If you knew me—if you knew—" He shakes his head, wrings his hands. "Well, the only thing I want here is justice."

Stone Phillips flips a page on his notepad, reads something, then leans in thoughtfully and says, "Mr. Marconi, are you referring to your client, or to the very recent death of your wife? Perhaps it might be helpful to our viewers to share a bit of personal information here, if you are willing."

Marconi shifts uncomfortably, and Stone turns to a cameraman offscreen and says, "Shut that off, will you, Mike? Let's go off the record for a minute, here."

The camera feed cuts out, then comes back on again.

Stone says to the camera, "My apologies to our viewers. We're not lying when we say we have no scripts for these things. At any rate, Mr. Marconi has agreed to make a brief statement."

The camera zooms in on Marconi's weary face.

"As I've made clear, it's not really relevant to the proceedings," he says, "and I don't care to speak much about the details. All I'll say is this: Yes, I lost my wife recently—a few weeks ago—to ovarian cancer. And my daughter, Hannah, and I, we—"

Marconi stops, choked up again, though you can tell he's frustrated with himself, that he wasn't intending to cry on national TV. It doesn't matter, though. I've heard enough. He just said *Hannah*. His daughter's name.

"My wife was not only a talented dancer in her own right, and the creative director for the New City Ballet, but she was the light of my life. The light of my daughter's life.

"And she and my daughter were both angry at me for taking this case. Yet, at the risk of their wrath, Stone, well, that is how very much I believe in this young man. How much I believe in his defense . . ."

Marconi's voice trails off, then returns, but I stop listening.

Her mother died months ago.

Around the time of Uncle Matt's accident.

And her father? What? I'm guessing he was in one of the Twin Towers.

But what if, by some chance, he wasn't?

Or what if he was, but made it out alive?

Isn't there a chance he could still be alive?

Then again, if he is alive, why isn't he looking for her? Why hasn't he found her yet?

I turn to the article in the magazine
        I slipped behind Kyle's sister's bed,
and stare at the boy's face.
       Harrison Highfront.
         Then
         I turn the page.
    Another inset photograph:
       My father on the courthouse steps,
       standing next to the kid.

I tear it out and
    shred it
    into a hundred
        tiny pieces.

I knock on the door, open it slowly.

She's sitting on Kerri's bed, her face wet with tears, pieces of paper torn and scattered around her.

"Hannah," I say.

She flinches and turns.

"I hated that case, Kyle," she blurts, "especially after my mother died. I hated the news cameras and interviews, hated how it made them both fight, and how he kept working on it no matter how ill she became. Even when she was dying. I hated what it made people believe about my father. But I realize this now: He really believed in the kid. And he was doing his job. God, he was just doing his job."

A sob escapes her throat, and she shakes her head as if she's refusing to let herself cry.

"And still, I screamed at him, Kyle. That very last morning when he headed off to work, I screamed at him. I said horrible, terrible things . . ."

She can't help it, begins to weep now, so I move toward her, to comfort her. But she turns away, her whole body wracked with sobs.

The tears come so hard I can't catch my breath,
    can't stop my body from shaking.

Kyle hugs me, and I fight him off.

I'm so angry and broken, I can't even bear to be hugged,

don't deserve to be hugged.

But then I give in, because I'm so,

so

lonely and

scared.

I let him wrap his arms around me as if I am good.

Let him hold me as if I am worthy of being held.

Which only makes me

cry harder.

"My mother is gone," I whisper through tears,

"and, now, my father is gone, too,

and I can never, ever fix the awful things I said."

Kyle rocks me as I sob and tells me kind things.

Says he knows,

says he understands,

says he promises.

Still, I can't stop crying.

I feel like I will never stop crying.

I pull her in tighter, not knowing what else to do.

Maybe I should get Dad to help.

Maybe I should get Uncle Matt.

Finally, I say, "Hannah, listen to me. I fight with my dad all the time. I say stupid shit I don't mean *all the time*. People do that when they're mad. When they're hurting. When they're sad. You didn't know—you couldn't have known—all the things that were going to happen on Tuesday. None of this is your fault. And I'm sure he knows you loved him. *Do love* him. Please, you don't know for sure that he's gone."

It takes a while, but she finally calms down, cries herself out or something. And when she does, she says, "You don't know, Kyle . . . but go ahead, type in his firm. There's no way . . ." She shakes her head. "No way he got out of there alive."

I walk her back to my room and we sit at my desk, each on half of my chair.

"You'll see, Kyle," she says, hiccuping back more tears. "Spencer and Marconi. Type it in and go to the site."

"Are you sure?"

"Yes. One World Trade Center. Please."

I type the names into the search engine, but my hands shake so much it takes me a minute to get it right. I keep hitting the wrong keys. When the links finally come up, I scan through them, praying there's no gruesome photo of her father. No missing persons poster, or obituary.

A bunch of links come up related to the Washington Square rape case, news stories and interviews, so it takes a minute for me to find the actual link for his law firm.

The Law Offices of Spencer and Marconi. When the page loads, his face—the face from TV—smiles out at me from a photo inset at the top. Hannah's breath hitches.

Next to Marconi is an older, white-haired man, heavyset, with a thick round nose and ruddy cheeks.

"That's John," she says, touching the screen. "He's very nice. A lot like an uncle to me." She sounds so sad, I can barely take it. "I'm guessing he's gone now, too." She points to the top of the page, the button that reads: *Contact us.* "Click on that," she says, her voice cracking.

When I do, the firm's telephone number and address pop up: One World Trade Center, 63rd floor. "See? That's where he works. That's where he was," she says.

Now I'm the one who can't breathe. I want to cry for her. I want to freeze-frame and reverse time, go back before I knew. Before I had any part in making her remember.

I wrack my brain. Cantor Fitzgerald, that big company that Bangor's uncle and Jenny Lynch's father worked for, was in the hundreds I think, like the 105th or 106th floor.

"The sixty-third floor is way below . . ." I start to say, but how do I phrase the rest without making myself cry or, worse, vomit? "Below where . . . Well, I bet a lot of people made it out of there."

I realize now from the photo on the website that it's the same office as the one Marconi was sitting in on *Dateline*, with the fancy mahogany conference table and the gold law books on the shelves behind him. And when the camera had panned out while Stone Phillips was talking to him? It had shown a wall of windows with a stellar view of downtown Manhattan.

"I know it's a long shot," I add, trying to sound positive, "but you shouldn't give up until we know for sure."

She nods, but a fresh stream of tears runs down her face. "I wish I hadn't fought with him, Kyle."

"You didn't know."

"But there's no excuse . . ." The tears turn to sobbing again, and she folds into me, lets me hold her and rock her some more. And, just when I think I may have her soothed, she says, "You don't understand, Kyle. I told him I hated him. I told him I wished he was dead instead of my mother."

WHERE ARE THE WINGS?

It takes me a long time after that to get her to calm down again. When I do, I say, "Come on, maybe we can find him. If anyone can, it's my dad. Let's go talk to him."

I stand, but she grabs my sleeve. "I can't do it, Kyle."

"Okay, then stay here. I will."

She nods, her lips pressed tight as she fights back a fresh wave of tears. "But first, before you do . . . I want to show you my mother."

He types your name,

     Danielle Marconi,

    the way I ask him to.

I say each letter aloud, though doing so

       makes me ache.

It hurts how much I miss you, Mom.

I do what she asks, even though it feels unbearable.
I do what she wants me to do.

I brace myself against the images that will come,

   though I've done this before, a hundred times since spring,
studied each detail of every photo,

    your face,

    your smile,

     your eyes.

   So many of them are copies of photos that hang on
our walls

in our home,
line our halls,
     rest on the credenza in my father's office.
       An office that is no longer there.
They are the photos of you that look out at me,
       your expression tricking me into believing
    that you may still
      be here.

When the links load, Hannah points to one and says, "That," so I click on the one that reads: PRINCIPAL DANCER/ CREATIVE DIRECTOR, NEW CITY BALLET.

She touches the screen as a photo appears—a photo of her, I mean, it's Hannah's face, only older—in a box in the upper right-hand corner. It is uncanny how much she looks like her mother. It's the same face I've been looking at for days.

Soft music plays, and a banner at the top of the page scrolls by:

NEW CITY BALLET MOURNS THE LOSS OF
OUR EXTRAORDINARY CREATIVE DIRECTOR
AND MUSE, DANIELLE "DANI" MARCONI.

"You look just like her," I manage.

She nods and bites her lip, causing a fresh spill of tears. She takes a deep breath and points to the words *Photo Gallery.* "Click on those," she says.

When I do, she looks away for a second. Pages of photographs slowly load, one after another. Tiny thumbnails that can be enlarged if you want to wait. In one after another, even small, I can pick out her mother, beautiful with her long black hair.

"Mine was long like that, too," Hannah says, touching the screen, laughing a little through her tears. "I shaved it with her, when hers started to fall out last winter. It grew back some, but I cut it off again. It's too—" She swallows. "I've been so angry . . . It's all so stupid," she says.

I turn and look at her, but, what am I supposed to say? What can I say that will make any of it better? I let my eyes scan the rows of photographs again, picking out her mother in each one.

In one she wears a long red gown, her hair pulled back into a jeweled bun. I touch the photo, and Hannah says, "That was two seasons ago, at her installation as Creative Director. It was an amazing night, after a performance of *Sleeping Beauty*." I nod, and she adds, "Not long before she was diagnosed."

In another, she wears a simple brown dress with a tie at the waist. She bows with a line of dancers at the front and center of the stage. In yet a third, she's dressed in costume, I think from *The Nutcracker*. I recognize it from Kerri's dance-school production, which was lame. But also because there's that giant red Nutcracker guy behind her.

In still one more, she's center stage in another fancy gown, but looking thin and pale, her hair short and wispy now. A group of dancers—men in white tights, women dressed in lots of white tulle—stands to each side of her in front of a raised platform designed with cattails and plumed grasses, surrounding what looks like real water.

"That was from Swan Lake," Hannah whispers.

And then I see Hannah. The one next to her mother curt-seying, in the center.

She wears a white costume with a tulle skirt and an elaborate headpiece covered in the same white feathers as the wings. The ones hanging from Kerri's chair.

I reach out and touch the screen again. "But where are the wings?" I ask, and she does the half laughing, half crying thing again.

"Oh, those weren't part of the costume, just for promotional purposes. But I liked to wear them . . . She used to call me her butterfly . . . You can't actually dance in those wings." She shakes her head, pulls a tissue from the box on my desk, and blows her nose.

"She was supposed to play Odette, the swan princess," Hannah explains. "But she was too weak to do it, so they let me go on for her. She got to see me dance the role. It was the last time she ever saw me dance."

LE PETIT PAIN

"We're at our café," I hear myself say,
        touching the photo on the screeen,
            the one of
            me,
            dressed as
                Odette.
    "In all my dreams, we're still there, on the lake
    on that stage,
    or at our little café.
    Our favorite French café on Vesey Street."
I get up and walk to his bed,
lie down,

and close my eyes.
I can't look at photographs anymore.

    "Come sit here," I say, "and I'll tell you."
    I'll tell you it all.
He does, and I let the memories
rush in.

I sit with her and hold her hand, and listen.

"Every Tuesday, we'd go there,
to that little café on Vesey Street.
    Le Petit Pain.
        Now it's probably buried
        beneath
    all that
    rubble."

Her voice trails off, but I get it all now. The whole picture is coming together. Vesey Street is right there. It literally runs into the Twin Towers.

"That was our thing," she continues, "a family ritual. My mom's favorite place in the world. They got married there." She looks at me and says, "In January, in the middle of a snowstorm, they got married in the courtyard there." I raise my eyebrows, and she explains. "Antoine—he's the owner—he had this temporary glass dome installed so it would stay warm for the wedding, for her. Of course I wasn't there, but I've seen photographs. The courtyard was covered in fruit trees, blooming in blue-glazed pots.

"Antoine loved my mother so much . . . For their last anniversary, my father and Antoine hung pale pink laterns from the beams," she says, her voice filled with melancholy now, "and covered the branches in sparkling white lights, just like at their wedding. It was magical. When I was little, I loved to page through their wedding album. They looked like figures inside a snow globe."

I see you there,
      caught in the flurry,
     all rosy cheeks and twinkling lights,
   your white dress with the fluffy white trim framing your face,
      baby's breath crowning your head.
I see you there, still,
    in your leotard and pink chiffon skirt,
        en pointe,
   all magic and grace.
    A jewel-box ballerina,
twirling forever inside my head.

She squeezes her eyes shut as if she's trying to keep in the tears, then lets go of my hand, and walks to my window.

"Every Tuesday, Kyle, like clockwork, we'd take the subway downtown from Grand Central together and eat breakfast at Antoine's café, in the courtyard."

"Le Petit Pain," I say, wanting her to know that I'll remember every detail.

She nods. "It means 'little bread.' Well, not little exactly, but, like, sweet little bread. And every Tuesday morning, Antoine, not the waiters, would serve my parents and me breakfast. But it was for her that he did it. He loved her so much. Everyone did."

"I bet," I say, my heart breaking for her.

"From there, my father would go to work, and my mother and I would head uptown to work, and to school."

"At LaGuardia," I say.

She turns fast, her eyes searching mine.

"How did you know?"

I walk back to my desk, slide open the drawer, and pull out the ribbon with the ballet slipper charm tied to the plastic sleeve with her tattered ID.

I hand it to her. Her face holds a million questions.

"I didn't know it was in there at first," I say. "In the washing machine. I washed it accidentally. By the time I realized and found it, I couldn't make out most of what it said. But I could make out the letters of the school, and, of course, a few of the letters in your name. Not enough of them, but still. Enough to know it was you, when I heard your father on TV . . . I probably should have told you sooner. I wanted to give you time."

She takes the ribbon from me and squeezes the charm in her hand. "It wouldn't have mattered," she says. "I'm glad to have this, though. I thought I'd lost it for good."

"Oeufs au nid."

My mother takes a small bite of the egg-soaked bread and smiles, making her eyes crinkle. "No one makes them like Antoine does, do they, Papillon?"

I shake my head, taking a bite of my own. "Except in Paris," I say, and she nods.

"Except in Paris," she says.

It's spring, two years before she will be diagnosed, the morning after I get my acceptance into the dance program. We're celebrating. Dad is here, too, though he can't stay as long. He'll head to work as soon as he's done eating.

"Tell me again about Paris," I say. "About the Paris Opera Ballet. *Swan Lake*, 1984. I love when you tell me your stories."

"Well now, Papillon, you've heard mine enough. Soon you will have stories of your own."

She reaches into her bag and pulls out a small teal box, tied with a silver-white ribbon. Inside is a pink pointe shoe charm.

"From Tiffany's," she says. "Your father and I, we're so very proud of you."

As she talks, my mind races. I want to get Dad, tell him what's going on, and see if he can find out more about her father.

"Give me a second. Wait here," I say. "I swear I'll be right back."

In the hall, so she won't see, I scrawl *John Marconi, Esq., Spencer & Marconi, 1 World Trade Center, 63rd floor* on a piece of paper, and run to his study.

He's on the phone, cups a hand over the receiver. "Sorry. It's kind of important," I say.

I hold out the scrap of paper to him, say breathlessly, "Her name is Hannah Marconi. John Marconi is her father. He's one of the lawyers for those prep-school kids. Harrison Highfront, remember? The Washington Square Park rape case. He worked in the Twin Towers."

For a second, my father's face is riddled with confusion, then he begins to register the information.

"I'll explain better later, " I say. ". . . there was a rerun . . . We saw him on TV . . ."

He holds up a finger to me, uncovers the phone. "Let me call you back, Paulie," he says.

"Okay, Kyle, tell me."

I nod, fighting back tears. "Her mom died last spring. Some kind of cancer. Ovarian, she said. And now her dad was in one of the towers. She thinks he's . . . I mean, probably he is, right? Because he was in there. But what if . . . ?" I look down, not wanting to say anything that will sound stupid or naive. I keep thinking of Dad saying I was getting too attached to the girl. "It wasn't those higher floors, though, so maybe . . . Can you check? I'm hoping maybe you can find him."

He stares at the paper and narrows his eyes, and I can see him calculating the possibilities. He glances at the clock. It's already late, well after eight P.M. "Let me call Butch," he says, "try to reach someone at the station. Maybe a Missing Persons call has come in. Now that we have a name, maybe we can find something."

"Thanks, Dad," I say. "Let me know as soon as you find him."

I go back to my room. The girl is standing at the window.

"Are you okay? My dad is looking for—for information. Tell me the rest now. I want to hear."

"It was a Tuesday, last October, and still summer-warm—warm enough to sit outside—when they told me she was going to die.

"She said the words, not my father. Told me she had stage-four ovarian cancer, and that they hadn't caught it in time.

"I didn't believe them, Kyle. I didn't want to. She was still so young. But it had already spread to nearly every part of her body.

"They gave her three months. She was so strong and brave.

"She lived for almost nine months more."

"And this Tuesday?" I ask.

"Yes, I'm getting to that," Hannah says.

"Even as she grew sicker, we continued to go down to Antoine's—Le Petit Pain—almost every Tuesday morning. Even as she worked less, and danced less, even as the chemo chemicals made her teeth hurt and took away all her beautiful hair.

"It's not that we were pretending she was okay, because we weren't. But she loved it there so much. If we could have, we would have spread her ashes there."

Kyle nods and holds my hand.

His hand feels so perfect in mine.

"And then, after she died, my father wouldn't go there anymore. He told me he couldn't bear the place. But I felt closest to her there. So I'd go without him, alone. What else was I going to do?

"I could feel her presence everywhere there. In the cobble-stones. In the glazed pots with their fruit trees. In the lanterns."

"It sounds magical," Kyle says.

"Yes," I say. "I think it was."

"Do you think he'll reopen it? Antoine, I mean."

She shrugs. "I hope so."

"So that's where you were Tuesday morning," I say. "In that courtyard, when the towers went down."

She nods, bites her lip. "After the second plane hit," she says, "I ran. I knew he was in there. I needed to get to my father."

Her voice breaks now, her words choked out by a fresh flow of tears.

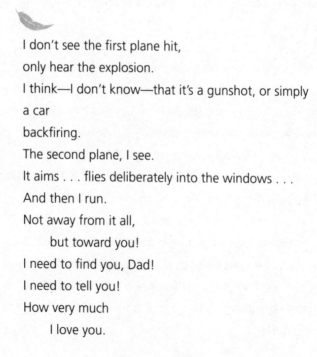

I don't see the first plane hit,
only hear the explosion.
I think—I don't know—that it's a gunshot, or simply
a car
backfiring.
The second plane, I see.
It aims . . . flies deliberately into the windows . . .
And then I run.
Not away from it all,
    but toward you!
I need to find you, Dad!
I need to tell you!
How very much
    I love you.

I don't know how long we sit there after that, just quiet, until Dad finally knocks on my door.

I search his expression for answers, but he's in detective mode, poker-faced, expression unreadable.

Hannah stands. She lets go of my hand.

"It's okay, Mr. Donahue, go ahead. You can tell me. I'm ready to know."

VII

NEWS

As my dad stands there, this lame old joke I once read in some kid's book runs through my head:

Doctor: I have some bad news and some very bad news.

Patient: Well, you might as well give me the bad news first.

Doctor: The lab called with your test results. They said you have twenty-four hours to live.

Patient: Twenty-four hours! That's terrible! What could be worse news than that?

Doctor: I've been trying to reach you since yesterday.

Dad clears his throat.

Hannah waits, brave and strong.

When he speaks, I'm surprised to hear his voice shaking.

"We found him, sweetheart, and he's alive. He's been in Roosevelt Hospital since Tuesday morning."

"He is?" The look on Hannah's face overwhelms me. Fear on top of panic on top of the most joyous kind of relief known to man. "Is he going to be okay?"

"He is. He suffered smoke inhalation and a concussion. A beam fell on him in the stairwell, near the very bottom of the stairs."

Dad chooses his words carefully, so I'm wondering if there's going to be some sort of bombshell. But then he smiles and says, "I spoke to him. He sounds strong and well. He woke up this morning, and discharged himself this afternoon. He has been trying to find you, to reach you, ever since. He's been calling the precincts like a madman."

Dad gives me a look here, but we both know it may not have made much of a difference. Either way, I close my eyes and breathe. I try to relax. Maybe for the first time since Tuesday.

"Wait, so he's alive and okay, Mr. Donohue?"

"Yes, he is," Dad says, smiling. "Any minute, he'll be on his way here to get you."

LATE FRIDAY NIGHT, 9.14.01

So, like that, it's over. At least the part with me and the girl with the wings.

Hannah.

She's gathering up her things to go home.

Dad nearly cries telling her the rest of the information. Honestly, I can't remember the last time I saw him so happy to deliver some news.

Hannah walks over to hug him and, as she does, for the first time since all of this happened, I remember the other news I have for him. The news about Uncle Matt. How he lifted his arm, moved his hand, all on his own. I forgot all about it in the chaos. I'll tell Dad soon. He'll be super excited to know.

"He said to warn you," Dad tells Hannah, "that he may look a little worse for the wear. He was seriously banged up, and his head is shaven, for the stitches, and he's got a few other souvenirs like that. But he's *okay*. That's the important thing. And he says he can't wait to see you." He cuffs her head. "He was beside himself to know that you're okay. I offered to drive you up tomorrow morning, but he said he wanted to get you now, tonight. I know some guys up there—" He turns to me now. "They live in Westchester. So I've called the captain, and he's getting someone from the five-two to bring him down tonight. They should be here before midnight."

Before midnight.

"Wait, Westchester?" I say, trying not to let the disappointment in my tone take away from anything. But, at the moment that sounds a million miles away.

"Yes. We had just moved there from the city, before my mother was diagnosed," Hannah says. "She was admired . . . I'm sure that's why my school let me stay . . ."

Her voice trails off, lost in some memory. I try to stay present and happy for her, to stop my mind from making the impossible calculations. *I'd have to take the train. There are no subways to Westchester.* Still, I'm happy for her. Seriously. Like, ridiculously happy. It's just too fast. We don't even have until tomorrow.

But I'm being selfish. She needs to see her dad. Of course she does. As soon as possible.

She needs to go home.

"Are you sure, Mr. Donohue?" she asks.

"Yes, believe me. It's been an awful few days. These guys will be happy to help, to be a part of a story with a happier ending."

LOFTY ASPIRATIONS

Dad closes the door and leaves us alone, but what do I do now, with the stupid little time we have left? Congratulate her? Kiss her? Make her prick her finger and rub her blood together with mine?

If I thought it might do anything, I would.

I sit on my bed, and she sits next to me.

We can pretend it's not over, and for a short time, we will. We won't admit what both of us know. We'll make all sorts of plans, and, for a while, maybe, we'll do our best to keep them. Plans to do what, I don't know. Go to a movie. Grab some pizza. All of it seems insignificant compared to what we've been through.

There's always the infamous penpals via e-mail. The dreaded *We will always be friends.*

But at sixteen, without a car or my license yet, Westchester is far enough from Brooklyn it might as well be Nebraska.

And even if we both go to school in the city, we're on opposite ends, and I'm guessing her dance schedule is intense—plus, nearly two hours is a heck of a long commute from here to there. Doable, yeah. But probably not for long.

Besides, I have this aching sense that what Hannah and I have is one of those things that happens in a vacuum, that can't be sustained under normal conditions. Under the pressures of school, and life, and parents, and siblings, and distance. It's something quiet and possessive, that will fall apart once it's diluted.

For example, at Jenny Lynch's father's funeral at the end of the following week, I'll decide to tell Marcus about her, or at least try, and he won't even really believe me.

Instead, he'll crack some lame joke about my imaginary friend, which Bangor will laugh at, too, even though he's at his second funeral in three days. I won't mind that he laughs, or that they both joke about her being some made-up figment of my very bored, very cooped-up imagination. An angel with wings, arisen from smoke and ash, visible to no one except me.

"Nice story, dude," Marcus will say. "You should be a writer."

"Let me guess, Donohue," Bangor will chime in. "She came

to you late at night, alone in your bed, slipped under the covers, and gave you a hand job. Until you figured out the hand was attached to you."

And I'll laugh, too, not because it's all that funny, but because I'm just so happy to be joking around. Because on a Tuesday morning less than two weeks ago, something happened so horrible it brought us to our knees. So horrible, it felt like we might never laugh again. And, for that reason alone, I won't try much harder to convince them.

But now, I'm still here, facing the prospect of Hannah leaving.

"I forgot to tell you," I say, staring as she folds my stuff and puts it on my bed. "Uncle Matt moved his arm earlier. He reached out and took a piece of cookie from my hand. So maybe he *is* getting better. Who knows? Maybe he'll even be walking soon."

She turns to me, genuine joy on her face. "That's awesome, Kyle. I bet you're right. I bet he absolutely will."

It's nearly eleven. My eyes keep going to the clock.

It's hard to trust that everything is okay.

Even with the police escort, the cars are getting stopped, so it's taking forever to get on and off highways and over the bridge to get to me.

The truth is, as long as he's okay,

I'm not in any rush for him to get here.

I carry my small pile of things, including the wings, into the living room, leave them on a chair, and sit on the couch next to Kyle. Out on the East River, the occasional flash from a police boat reflects off the water.

I squint through the haze in the dark, but it's too hard to

see anything through the smoke, to find the gap in the skyline
where two majestic buildings used to be.

"I keep thinking about that first night," I say to Hannah,
"when you said you didn't remember about the buildings. Do
you remember that now?"

It's a half-assed question. Part of me wants to know how
much she knew, and when, but mostly, I guess, it doesn't matter.

"Yes," she answers softly. One word that doesn't give too
much away.

"Well, I'm glad you were here. And I'm glad we got to hang
out and everything. I wish you didn't have to go home."

"Me, too, Kyle," she says. "Though I will be glad to see my
father."

"Of course you will," I say. "I'm glad for that, too."

I get up for a second, needing to collect my thoughts. I go off to
find Dad. I want to tell him about Uncle Matt and see if Mom
has made any progress getting home.

I find him in Uncle Matt's room, getting him ready for
bed.

He looks beyond tired, as if the past few days have aged him
a freaking decade.

"I should help more here," I say, walking around to give
him a hand with the sleeve of Uncle Matt's pajama shirt. "I
mean, on normal days from now on. Pick up the slack like I've
done this week. I know how hard it is, and maybe I've been
afraid to try, to help. But I'm good at it now, right, Uncle Matt?
And he's doing much better, so it makes it easier to help him."

I walk to the other side of the wheelchair. "I'll take this side. It will be quicker with both of us moving him."

Dad looks up at me now, his eyes softer. "Thanks. That'd be really great, Kyle."

I stand at the window, let my eyes take in Lower Manhattan, still muted by the endless haze of smoke.
Somewhere well north of here is the expanse of Westchester, and home.
She's not there, my mother,
            and I miss her.
        It's a hard, choking kind of missing that doesn't go away.
I'm going to miss Kyle, too,
            a more gentle kind of missing.
But in that direction, north, the lights shine crisp and clear.

On my way back to the living room, I stop briefly in my room and grab my PopMart Tour T-shirt she left folded on the bed.

I flip on the television and turn it to Comedy Central.
Cow and Chicken is on.
"Look what I found," I say, smiling, when Kyle walks back into the room.

"Fitting," I say, sitting on the couch next to her. "It's the episode where Cow wants to be a ballerina." I think about taking her hand, but I don't. I'm not sure I can handle it right now. Or at least handle the part where I have to let it go again. "She wants to be a ballerina, but she's clumsy. So she keeps tripping and breaking things."

"Well, she *is* a cow," Hannah says. "So those are some lofty aspirations."

I smile, and she turns and looks at me, a look I can't explain except to say that it burns through me, leaving a permanent afterimage. It's a look I will never forget. A look I don't want to forget.

I take a deep breath, then reach over and place my PopMart Tour T-shirt in her lap.

"I want you to have this," I say.

"Are you sure?"

"Yes."

She hugs the shirt to her chest and closes her eyes. On the screen, Cow is comically dancing away.

I say, "Poor Cow's mom, she's trying to protect her from Red Guy. You can see why, too. She's going to end up embarrassed."

As if to agree, Cow's mom says to her dad, "She's not ready, can't you see?"

Then Cow's dad looks at her and says, "Sometimes never being ready is the best kind of ready to be."

Hannah says, "Did you hear that, Kyle?"

I nod, and she laughs and squeezes my hand, then, better still, she moves closer and rests her head on my shoulder.

"That's the truth, isn't it?" she says.

VIII

WHAT SUSTAINS US

My father isn't allowed to drive, isn't even supposed to be discharged, so the officer drives, steering the car over the bridge and onto the highway.

In front of us, another squad car with its red lights flashing, silently leads the way.

My breath hitches as Brooklyn disappears in the rearview mirror.

When he first got to Kyle's, my father told Kyle and Mr. Donohue as much as he could manage about that morning. How the building had trembled when the first plane hit, followed by a series of smaller explosions. How things had popped and broken, shook and rumbled above him. How, by the time he got to the stairwell, there was a logjam of people inching their way down in the dark. How everyone was terrified but calm.

His voice caught. "Everyone was helping everyone," he said.

And, how, near the bottom, there was another explosion that rocked everything, and the stairwell around him crumbled, and it all went black.

"That was the last thing I remember," he said.

He explained how rescue workers must have carried him out, as well as the woman who was with him.

He turned to me then, tears in his eyes, and told me how the first thing he did when he woke up in the ICU was ask for me, how panicked he was to call everywhere and not be able to find me.

But he said, too, that he knew I was smart, and had faith I was safe, that someone kind had taken me in.

And that he knew I'd been upset, and had prayed over and over again that I'd simply gone to stay with a friend.

It broke my heart when he said that, admitted he was terrified when it seemed as if I wasn't even looking for him.

In the car, at first, he asks me a lot of questions, ones I can't answer, or ones I'm not ready to try. Not here, now, with the police officer in the car. After a while, he seems to get it, and we sit in silence. It's enough to be going home together.

Once in a while, I catch him glancing at my reflection in the window. A few times, he turns around and smiles.

Are you okay? his eyes ask. I know that's what he wants to know.

And I guess I am. What are my choices? What else am I going to be other than okay?

I turn and stare out the window, my reflection bouncing back at me in the dark. Lit staccato by the passing streetlights.

Each time I reappear, I see you, Mom.

My face is yours. My eyes are yours.

The hair that will grow back is yours.

It catches me off guard.

And, it sustains me.

"You have my talent, too," I can still hear you say.

With every breath, new memories flood in. From the past few days. From last year. From what feels like another lifetime.

Like one from a particular morning in spring, when I'm so, so little, and you slip into bed next to me, cuddle me close, and tell me how happy I make you.

Then you pull the sheets up over our heads like a tent, and you say, "Watch this," and you shake them hard so they billow up high like a parachute, then come floating magically down.

And, another, from a sunny afternoon in your dusty studio, the very first time you teach me the *pas de deux* from *Swan Lake*. You wrap your arms around me from behind, hold my arms out, and move them, and we walk through the choreography together.

"You're my shadow," you say. "My perfect little butterfly.

My *peu papillon*."

The memories drift back, clear
          and welcome,

as if on bird wings,

to

alight

      in my heart.

After she's gone, I follow Dad back to his study. It's midnight here, and nine P.M. in California. He tells me that Mom and Kerri will be on the red-eye flight home.

I say, "I wanted to tell you this before, but I didn't have the chance," and I tell him about Uncle Matt. I tell him about the decks of cards he's recited from memory, about the loci tricks he can still do, and, most importantly, about how, this evening, he moved his arm without my help.

Dad stares down for a second, the look on his face hard to read. As if he's calculating, doing some math problem in his head.

"Are you sure, Kyle?" he finally asks.

"I am," I say.

He nods, and I wait for him to say something more, to be

excited, and thrilled, and joyful, but all he does is nod again, before returning to whatever has his attention.

And I'm about to be furious, to scream and yell and tell him off, tell him how he needs to be more supportive of Uncle Matt. But then it hits me. Maybe because of something I can see in his expression, or something I feel in his effort to stay silent that I never noticed before: His silence isn't callous. It's protective. Not just of me, but of himself.

He doesn't want to get my hopes up, or his own.

"I'm not naive," I say, making my voice softer, but keeping my delivery confident and strong. "I get that he may never walk again, and I'll deal with that. We all will. But maybe the doctors are right and the swelling is still going down. Maybe there's a lot more progress he can make. Maybe he will walk again. And maybe he won't. But it's possible. And that's worth something. And he's seeming a lot more like his old self."

Dad nods again and picks up the phone. His eyes are damp in the corners. "I should call Paulie. Fill him in. And find out the best way to deal with the airport."

"Okay," I say, and I walk toward the door. But then, I stop again.

"And, Dad?"

"Yes?"

"I mean it. I'm going to help around here a lot more. I want to. But, we need to keep Uncle Matt here."

I walk with my father into our dark, empty house.

It's so quiet. I feel her here, sense her here, in everything we own. I'm sure he does, too.

I kiss him good night.

"I love you, Hannah," he says.

"I love you, too, Dad. And I'm sorry. I need to say that. I'm so very glad you're okay."

In my room, I put my few things down, then sit, holding my palm to my bedside lamp. I stare at the lines where they crisscross, at the island where Madame Yvette pressed her finger, where the lifeline veers and breaks.

The place of great tragedy, where Kyle and I will always connect.

I open my other palm, where I wrote his e-mail address. It's smudged from sweat, but I can still make out all the letters.

Smiling, I pick up his blue T-shirt, the one that says PopMart, with the planet that's not a planet, and slip it on, and crawl into my own bed.

I don't sleep much, hear Dad get up early and shower, leaving for the airport before dawn. He should be back with Mom and Kerri soon.

I keep thinking about the timing of everything. It's like Hannah and Kerri and my mom will be those proverbial ships that pass in the night. Some sort of cryptic Zen koan.

Besides me, Uncle Matt is the only one who truly knew her.

Not that Dad hasn't caught Mom up, told her everything, but he doesn't really know her either. Not like we do. Not like I do.

If a tree falls in the forest and you're not there to hear it, does it really make a sound?

I flip my pillow to the cool side, and stare around my room. Her fingerprints are here. The pillow smells the way the vanilla had smelled, so much better in her hair.

And, in the corner by my closet, my electric guitar is out and waiting, now propped against the wall. Tomorrow I'll practice some pieces for jazz band. In my head, I run through the chords to some of the songs I used to know how to play. With time, I'm sure it will all come back to me.

I close my eyes and picture her here—Hannah—on my bed, listening to me play. I try to hold on to how it felt to have her listen, how it felt to kiss her, and to hold her hand in mine.

Over and over, I think of her wading into the Atlantic.

"It's like I'm here, solid, but I'm not connected to anything. I'm completely untethered."

"You're tethered to me," I say aloud.

Out in the hall, the sound of bags dropping, a key in the lock, and my parents' hushed voices. I roll onto my stomach, hang my arm over the side of the bed, and pretend to be asleep.

"I've got the bags, Alyssa. Let go." Dad, as always, wanting to do everything.

The door opens, and Kerri's voice bursts in. "Hush!" Mom whispers. "You'll wake your brother. Seriously, Tom, leave them here. We'll unpack it all later."

The door closes, and Dad drops the bags obediently. I change my position, pull the covers over my head, and play possum like I used to when I was little. I'm not ready to talk with anyone yet.

"Go straight to your room, Kerri," Mom whispers again. "You can nap, and I'll wake you in a few hours." To Dad: "She was petrified, Tom. I couldn't get her to sleep a wink on the plane."

Dad says, "Can't say I blame her. I haven't really slept much, either." There's a pause, and the sound of bodies shifting, then footsteps moving down the hall. "Come on, pipsqueak," Dad says to my sister. "I'll tuck you in. You need to get some shut-eye."

I hear Dad walk her to her room. Her door opens and then, a few minutes later, closes again.

Later, when we wake for the day, when we shower and all sit at the kitchen table, our house will be normal again. The girl won't be down the hall.

Hannah.

I lift off the blankets and hold my hand to the light from the window. On my palm, scrawled across the lifeline, is her phone number.

I close it in a fist, sensing movement at my door, the presence of my mom in the hall.

My doorknob turns, and the door cracks open. She slips in and walks to my bed.

"Kyle?"

"Unh," I mumble incoherently, rolling away to face the wall. I'm hoping she'll buy that I'm sleeping.

She leans down, presses her hand to my back, then reaches to touch my cheek.

"I'm so glad you're okay," she whispers. "So grateful. I hear you did a tremendous job. I love you so very much." Her voice cracks a little at the end.

"Me, too, Mom," I offer sleepily. I don't want to talk, but I need her to know that I do. "I love you, too," I add.

I need her to know that, and that I'm happy she's home safe and sound, and that Kerri and Dad are, too.

Honestly, I'm still a little scared.

About tomorrow, and the day after that.

About next week, and when school will reopen, and where. Worried about whether we'll get hit again, and what might happen in the city.

But for right now, we're all okay, and here, together. And it's kind of amazing to be tethered. To have a face I belong to.

Author's Note

It's a beautiful Tuesday morning in September. My older son is in his first-grade classroom, and I've just dropped my younger son off at his Long Island preschool when I emerge to an onslaught of anxious chatter in the parking lot. Something unusual has happened in New York City.

I don't stick around to find out what. I have work to do and only a few hours before it's time to pick up my toddler again. I get back in my car and switch on the news.

A freak accident: A plane has flown into the North Tower of the World Trade Center.

By the time I reach home and turn on the television, a second plane has hit the South Tower, and no one is talking about accidents anymore.

I was only two years old in 1966 when my father, a young surgeon, was drafted into a MASH unit in Vietnam. He returned a year later, and I came of age in the relative peace and insulation of the post–Vietnam War America of the 1980s and 1990s. Now, less than fifty miles from my idyllic Long Island home, in the city where I lived for nearly a decade after college—a city I love—all that I know is unraveling.

I frantically call my husband at his law firm, twenty miles closer to the chaos. It is still early enough that many people don't know, so the phone lines aren't yet jammed. But when he answers, the enormity of the tragedy becomes palpable. The younger brother of a close colleague of his works at Cantor Fitzgerald, a company located precisely where the first plane hit.

My husband heads home as the news escalates, reported with a swift, unchecked panic the likes of which I've never seen before. On-air reporters break down despite efforts to maintain their composure. The Pentagon has been hit; the Twin Towers have gone down one after another; a plane bound, reporters believe, for the White House has crashed in a field in Pennsylvania. Because the government fears more attacks, military jets are scrambled, U.S. airspace is cleared with an order to shoot down unauthorized planes, and the death toll, later reduced by more than half, is reported likely to top six thousand.

Are more attacks coming?

Are we at war?

I manage to locate my sister, who still lives in Manhattan, then race to gather my boys from their schools.

I don't remember what I said when I pulled them from class, but I do remember what we did when we arrived home: We played Wiffle ball on our front lawn.

I know this sounds incongruous, but it was a picture-perfect day here on Long Island, and my primary goal at that moment was to shield my children from my fear. I knew I could not go back into our house and turn on the news, risking the carnage they might see. The broadcast images were terrifying: Buildings imploding, collapsing, pieces raining down like confetti. People bloodied, covered in dust and ash, running from that impossibly huge wall of barreling white smoke . . .

So, under azure, cloudless skies, on a warm pre-fall morning as our world forever changed, the boys and I played Wiffle ball, and I fought to keep my eyes from darting to now wholly untrustworthy skies.

As the months passed, and we all began to share and heal, it became clear that the irony of the weather was not lost on a single New Yorker that day.

Life stabilized. I returned my boys to their schools and daily routines, went back to my own part-time legal work and writing, vacuumed the house, read books, and made dinner plans with friends. But, for more than a year, I remained terrified in a way I had never before known.

And, through it all, what was there to do but keep moving?

So we did. We went to school and work, we played games and made pancakes for breakfast, we forged onward. Even as anthrax scares escalated, the threat of war grew, and the post-9/11 statistics staggered us all.

Over 2,700 people lost their lives on 9/11, at least 343 of whom were firefighters and paramedics, and twenty-three of whom were NYPD police officers. In the years following, those numbers have nearly doubled due to cancers and illnesses believed to be related to the tragedy. In the months after 9/11, only 291 bodies were recovered intact from Ground Zero. Nearly two thousand families received no remains whatsoever. Fires burned at the site for at least ninety-nine days, and the estimated economic loss to New York was more than $105 billion.

The statistics were mind-boggling, but they weren't all horrifying.

On 9/11, there were more than thirteen thousand babies born in the United States amid a rising death toll. And in the days after, at least thirty-six thousand units of blood were donated to the New York Blood Center. New Yorkers proved to be resilient—a resiliency rate quoted by mental health professionals to be better than 65 percent in the months after 9/11— and general suicide rates six months post-9/11 decreased significantly.

But statistics can't illustrate the sense of unity that blanketed our nation in a way not felt since immediately after World War II. We moved forward boldly, and we did it together.

At some point, my writer's brain started to whisper a mantra:

Write about it. Tell a story that might help you to bring the incomprehensible under control. A story about how we keep going, keep moving forward. How we heal.

The Memory of Things eventually became that story.

I didn't start the story right away. Not for years, in fact. In my heart, I knew it was too soon. Too soon for me to try to write it, too soon for others to read it.

But, in time, the images started to come.

The girl came first, crouched in fear.

Covered in ash.

On her back, a pair of playful costume wings.

And a boy. A boy who might save himself by having to save her first.

Make it a simple story about hope.

Make it a story about human resilience.

Make it a story where people still laugh, still brush their teeth, still fall in love, a story where people redeem one another by small gestures, a story where people have no choice but to keep going in the face of huge tragedy and unspeakable loss.

I know the events of 9/11 are fiercely personal to each and every one of us, and, as such, I know—and fear—I cannot begin to do justice to individual experiences on that day, or to the loss of human life that came with it. Through this story, I can only grapple with my own experiences, and my own memories of that moment in time, as flawed as those memories necessarily are as the years pass.

I ask my readers to remember that the story within these pages is pure fiction. Though I have taken great care to sift through countless articles, time lines, and brutal photographs from the day, as well as having the manuscript vetted by a police officer (who was also, at the time, a young mother) sent down to the Twin Towers that morning, I have taken liberties, too, as we do when we are writing fiction. In the end, this is nothing more than Kyle Donohue's story. A story about a boy who has to hold it together during one week amid a swirl of unthinkable tragedy he is forced to deal with on his own.

Ultimately, this is not a 9/11 story, but a coming-of-age story, one about healing and love. Still, I have tried to capture some of the sights and sounds and fears of that day—especially here in New York—and, more importantly, the astounding sense of camaraderie and resilience that we all experienced, and have tried to hold on to, in the days that followed.

This is a story about hope.

Acknowledgments

Books, like so many difficult endeavors, take a village to get from idea to well-told story to book on the shelf. This one was no exception. In this regard, my deepest gratitude to the following:

To Kathleen Coletti, Sergeant NYPD (retired), then also a young mother with young children at home on Long Island, who so bravely evacuated people from the towers that morning, and who read my manuscript with such great care to help shape and vet the important details of the story.

To Jane Small, for reaching out to tell me how the brief excerpts I shared on Facebook had made her want to read more, significant because it was the first time since 2001 (when she, herself, weathered the tragedy from mere blocks away) she had a desire to read a "9/11" story . . . then, for reading the manuscript again and again through every menial chore, to get to the heart of the story, and for making me believe others would find—and love—the heart of the story, too.

To my other first-round Beta readers: my mother, Ginger (who paints the way I only hope to write one day), blogger and reader extraordinaire Kelly Hager (a constant friend and cheerleader), and my dear friend Annmarie Kearney Wood (who always reads fast and makes me believe I have something worth pursuing). And, my second-round Beta readers: Evelyn Cruise (whose wonderful insight pushed me to be more careful and thoughtful), Cathy Burger Montiero (who read enthusiastically and gave me much-needed gold stars), Jessie Grembos (for all her amazing feedback and multiple reads), and Wendy Watts Scalfaro (who read at least twice with great care and encouragement).

To Robin Reul for her extraordinarily astute (and, thus, painful) notes. Oh, how we need those, especially from those we admire!

To Chris Lupone and Krysiek, aka "Polish Chris," for vetting the Polish words in the manuscript.

To Nicole, Meadow, and Brayden, for walking the neighborhood bridge with me to make sure I got it all right.

To the members of #TeachersWrite, who so often return my enthusiastic shake of pompoms with so much of the same; to my Facebook peeps, who read excerpts on a weekly basis and click "like" or, now, "love," and/or leave me endless words of encouragement that do matter; to the members of The West Neck Pod, who keep my body flowing without which no words would flow; and to the members of the Nerdy Book Club, who spread more book love than any other group on the face of this twirling planet.

To Ben R., for giving the manuscript so much of your time and skill, and, more so, for encouraging me to let the book be what I had always wanted it to be . . .

To Jim McCarthy, hugely, for getting and appreciating what I do, believing in my ability to ultimately do it well, for always reading and being available, and pushing me until the story is all he knows it can and should be.

To Vicki Lame, the Brave, for wanting it and getting it, period, like the badass she is, and for more than words could ever do her justice. In fact, please edit these. I love and admire you like crazy.

To David Curtis, for The Most Beautiful Cover of my Wildest Dreams.

And, to the team at St. Martin's Griffin, including Brandt, Peter, Jessica, Karen, Annie, and countless others I haven't yet met, who I know, as I type, are working tirelessly to get this story into the hands of readers because they believe it is worthy and important.

Lastly, of course, to my family, and, especially, David, Sam, and Holden, who always inspire me to be better, and to do better, and to make you all proud; and to my sister, Paige, and all the others who live in New York City who carried on with their day-to-day living in those early, terrifying, smoke-and-tear-filled days after we were hit.

If I have missed someone important, please know you have my undying thanks, and that it is not because your input didn't matter vastly and completely, but rather because neither my memory nor organizational skills have weathered how very long it took to write and revise this book, and get it to publication.

May you always be tethered.